No

Har...

romance
by Anne Mather
comes to life
on the movie screen

starring
KEIR DULLEA · SUSAN PENHALIGON

Leopard
in the
Snow

Guest Stars
KENNETH MORE · BILLIE WHITELAW

featuring GORDON THOMSON as MICHAEL
and JEREMY KEMP as BOLT

Produced by JOHN QUESTED and CHRIS HARROP
Screenplay by ANNE MATHER and JILL HYEM
Directed by GERRY O'HARA

An Anglo-Canadian Co-Production

Hawk in a Blue Sky

by

CHARLOTTE LAMB

Harlequin Books

TORONTO • LONDON • NEW YORK • AMSTERDAM • SYDNEY

Original hardcover edition published in 1977
by Mills & Boon Limited

ISBN 0-373-02161-5

Harlequin edition published May 1978

CHAPTER ONE

AMANDA BRYCE was riding a silver horse when she caught sight of a familiar face among the crowd thronging the Bank Holiday fair on Hampstead Heath.

For a dizzy second she felt almost as if the merry-go-round had whirled her back through time. The blaring music played on, the bright lights flashed, the horses went up and down, round and round. Amanda clung to the gaily painted, twisting pole which held her horse and thought about Cesare Druetso, the autocratic master of San Volenco, the medieval walled city from which she had fled five years ago.

Was it possible that here, among this noisily democratic London crowd, she was face to face with Cesare's brother Piero?

The music slowed. The merry-go-round slid to a stop. Five years were erased as Piero leapt to her side to help her to dismount, his dark eyes full of laughing warmth.

'I couldn't believe my eyes!' he greeted her. 'Of all the people in London you were the one I most wanted to see, and there you were, suddenly! It is incredible!'

Amanda could only murmur faintly, 'Piero ... is it really you?'

He kissed her hand with Latin gallantry. 'It is certainly me, and I am enchanted to see you again...'

'Goodness, you've grown up,' said Amanda, grinning.

'You were a hobbledehoy when I last saw you, but you've somehow managed to acquire the Druetso charm in the meantime, I see.'

'Hobbledehoy?' Piero's excellent English was not quite perfect, she saw, as he frowned enquiringly. 'It sounds revolting. Is it?' Then, seeing how she laughed, 'Yes, I see it is! And as for charm, I seem to remember you were proof against our family charm?' He flipped a thin dark brow upwards, looking amused.

She felt her cheeks flush and eyed him reproachfully. 'I don't think we should talk about that.'

'Why not? Everyone knew, even the hobbledehoy ... that is the word?' He was teasing her, enjoying himself. She remembered very well what a tease Piero had always been, a gay, good-humoured boy with eyes that twinkled and a mouth which smiled all the time. 'Imagine you turning Cesare down! The city buzzed with it for months! All the girls green with envy, thinking you mad ... not one of them would have missed the chance to marry my brother.'

'What are you doing in England?' She was determined not to discuss the matter. 'Have you been here long? When do you go back?'

He grimaced. 'O.K. I'm over here to learn the English end of the wine trade. I arrived last month and I go back in two months' time.' He stopped at a shooting gallery. 'Shall I win you a fluffy pink rabbit?' He beckoned to the attendant, selected a rifle and took aim. He was, she saw, a good shot. A few moments later they strolled away with a pink rabbit.

She eyed it with amusement. 'I'll always treasure it—it will remind me of you.'

'Hmm . . .' He gave her a thoughtful look. 'I've an idea I am going to have trouble with you. You use words like concealed weapons.'

She laughed. A sidelong glance reminded her of his dark Druetso looks, the clear olive skin, black curly hair and handsome features. As a boy she recalled him being extremely attractive—he had grown into a young man who captured all feminine eyes. He still bore the softness of youth about him, a faintly tender look about the mouth, an almost feminine delicacy. Remembering his brother, she guessed this would wear away with time. Cesare had been tougher, more angular in feature, a very masculine man.

Piero sobered. 'I was very sorry to hear about your father. We all were. We hoped you would come home after the funeral—my mother had your room ready.'

Gently, she said, 'England is my home now. It has been for the last five years.'

'But you are still half Italian,' he reminded her. 'You lived at Volenco for your first eighteen years. Doesn't that give us more of a claim than England?' He sounded hurt.

She smiled at him soothingly. 'I haven't forgotten Volenco, but I have made a life for myself here. I work in a large importer's office, translating Italian into English, and back again. I've a nice flat, friends, hobbies. I like London. There is always so much to do here.'

'So I have discovered,' he nodded. 'Will you come out with me now and then?'

She thanked him gravely. They stood together, in the anonymous shelter of the crowd, the lights flashing gaily around them, music soaring up into the London sky. Beyond the bright circle of the fair the Heath fell away, shadowy and mysterious, a natural oasis in London's vast sprawl. 'How odd that we should meet here!' She was astonished by the vagaries of fate.

'I rang you a couple of times,' Piero said. 'You were never in and I didn't leave my name because I wanted to surprise you.'

'I would have rung you back if you had,' she pointed out.

He shrugged, very Italian. 'It would have been less fun. And if you were very busy with someone...' His dark eyes probed her face, curious and shrewd. 'If there had been a man! You might not have wished to complicate things.'

Amanda gave him a long look. 'We grew up together ... we're almost brother and sister! Of course I wanted to see you, silly.'

'Brother and sister?' Piero made a fierce grimace. 'No, never that, *mia cara*.' And the soft outline of youth seemed harder, more masculine as he frowned.

'There are so many questions,' she said. 'So much I want to ask you. I hardly know where to begin.'

'You do not begin with Cesare?' he asked softly.

She flushed. 'How is Cesare?' She kept her tone light and cool.

'He is ... Cesare!' Piero laughed. 'He is, of course, unmarried still.'

'Why of course?' She pretended bafflement. 'Why shouldn't he have married in five years? With all those girls pining for him?'

'If he had married, Mamma would have written to you,' Piero pointed out calmly. 'She writes regularly, doesn't she? We see her letters going off to England every week, and letters coming back ... rather thin little envelopes compared to hers, but replies of a sort.'

She flushed. 'I have so little to tell her. My life...' She looked around her, half wildly. 'What can I tell her? What would she understand of London? She has never left Volenco in her life.'

Piero sighed. 'True.' He smiled at her, his dark eyes alight. 'But I shall have something to tell her in my next letter! Something to please her. She has always been so fond of you, Amanda *mia* ...'

'I'm very fond of her, too,' Amanda said eagerly.

'But not of Cesare?'

She was irritated. 'I wish you would stop harping on about your brother!' She was aware that her face was very pink, and that made her even crosser. Even at this distance, it seemed, Cesare could dominate the lives of those near and dear to him, and even the lives of those who detested him, as she did.

'Why *did* you refuse him?' Piero persisted, untroubled by her little tantrum.

Before she could stop herself she had retorted with the truth, 'I didn't want to marry a dictator!'

Piero looked astonished, amused, curious. 'A dictator?' He repeated the word as though it pleased him, savouring it.

'Cesare is an autocrat, the ruler of a tiny kingdom. His wife would be nothing but a slave.'

Some expression in Piero's dark eyes made her pause, a little anxious now. She was, after all, talking about his brother, and the Druetso family were so close. What affected one, affected all. They were always concerned for each other, involved with each other. That had been another reason for her father's decision to leave the city.

James Bryce had visited San Volenco after the war, met and fallen in love with the Conte's second cousin, a slight, fragile girl with black eyes and a sweet smile. They had married, and to please his wife James had settled in the city. He had run an antique shop. Their only child, Amanda, had been born and brought up there. Lucia Bryce had been entirely devoted to her daughter, but it had been her dearest wish to see Amanda married to the young Conte, Cesare. Cesare's mother, the Contessa Maria, had been Lucia's best friend since their schooldays together.

On Amanda's eighteenth birthday Contessa Maria had given a great party for her, in the castle hall, and afterwards Cesare had taken her to walk in the shadowy walled garden, where tubs of scarlet flowers made the air fragrant. Cesare had made a formal proposal, his dark face shuttered. Amanda, pale and stammering, had uneasily refused him. For a second he had stood quite still, then, looking up swiftly, she had seen his face unmasked, the habitual calmness he showed the world dissolved. Rage, black and terrible, flared out at her. She had backed away, trembling. She had not for a moment suspected this—it terrified her.

When they returned to the hall, everyone looked at them, and now she saw quite clearly that they all expected him to announce their engagement. The family had viewed it as a settled thing. No wonder poor Cesare had been furious—a public humiliation for him must have been galling, indeed.

Her mother's pain had been the worst to bear, particularly as, unknown to her, Lucia had been seriously ill then, and was to die shortly afterwards.

Amanda had felt sick with guilt after her mother's death, bitterly aware that she might have made her happy if she had accepted Cesare. If only he had been different! All her life she had been subject to Cesare's authority. He had been ten years her senior, a thin dark boy who seemed grown up when she was still a child and who settled naturally into his father's place on the old Conte's death. Amanda had, quite simply, been afraid of Cesare—an arrogant, ruthless man so much older than herself was not her idea of a romantic partner.

I was far too young, she thought now. Why had they all planned such an unsuitable match, anyway?

Why had Cesare agreed to it? she suddenly wondered. He was not the man to do anything unless he wished to do it, yet he had proposed obediently at his mother's suggestion! Presumably he had decided she would make a suitable bride, and had cared very little whether they could be happy. She could not imagine Cesare under the spell of emotion, blindly in love or weak at the knees, as she had been since once or twice.

Love had come to her briefly, violently. A tennis coach with sandy hair and strong, brown wrists ... a boy in Scotland last year, with heathery eyes and a delicious accent which thickened when he spoke shyly of love. Each had been mere episodes in her life, and she had known even in her brief delirium that it was not to last, but it had, in an odd sort of way, taught her much about love.

She suspected that Cesare had never even learnt that little. One had to abandon oneself, surrender, become weak. Cesare would never submit to that.

Piero was staring at her. 'What are you thinking about?'

She laughed. 'Nothing! It will be nice to talk to someone from Volenco again, that's all.'

She shared her three-roomed flat with two girl friends. They were capable, friendly, sympathetic girls, and Piero bowled them over. They could not take their eyes from his fine olive features, his beautiful mouth and dark eyes. He showed them his charm. his attentive courtesy. They sighed for vanished days of female subjection, then went off to do complicated, highly paid jobs, banishing Piero and his old-world attitudes from their minds. They knew their own world, and delightful as he was, Piero would not fit into it. He was a visitor from another time.

Several times a week after that Piero and Amanda

met, dined and danced, went to the theatre or concerts, walked in Kew Gardens or cruised up the River Thames. They saw most of London's sights together, did all the 'tourist' things which are so pleasurable despite the sophisticated jokes about them.

It was Sue who asked her, 'Are you falling for him, Mandy?'

And Amanda had looked startled, taken aback. 'What? How ludicrous!'

Sue had eyed her wryly. 'Sure?'

Then Piero, as they danced in a quiet club, held her closer and said with sudden huskiness, 'Amanda? *Cara?*'

She felt her knees suddenly weaken, recognised a familiar sense of subjection, a loss of identity. Surely not, she told herself fiercely. She had grown out of these adolescent crushes, these sudden attacks of love. Like the measles they were part of her youth. She was a grown-up now.

At the flat, deserted by her friends this evening, Piero kissed her, and the world spun like the merry-go-round at the fair. Amanda clung, her arms around his neck, while he whispered in Italian, the familiar words new-minted for this new love. '*Cara, cara* ... you're so beautiful, *tanto bella* ... I think I'm falling in love.'

At the back of her dizzy head a little voice said, 'No ... no!' But Amanda barely heard, did not comprehend. She was too busy coping with a rush of emotion.

Some weeks later they spent a Saturday at Kenwood House, in Hampstead, strolling in the landscaped gardens by the lake, viewing the paintings in the elegant eighteenth-century rooms, talking as they sunbathed on the lawns. They ate salad for lunch in the whitewashed coach-house, turned into a restaurant in these tourist-conscious days. Their table stood beside a well-preserved Victorian family coach, painted black and red. Amanda saw Piero's face reflected in the polished wood.

'Will you marry me?' he asked abruptly, leaning forward, his dark eyes intent. 'Come home, *cara*, home to Volenco, as my wife.'

There was a trance-like silence as she let the words sink into her brain. She had half anticipated them, yet she was still dumbfounded that he had actually said them.

She looked at him nervously. 'Piero ... it's so difficult ...'

'Cesare?' He looked back gently. 'I know, but after five years it is unlikely he will mind at all. Everyone will be happy to have you back. Especially Mamma ... I have hinted in my letters, and I think she guesses. I am sure they will accept it.'

There was no need for him to ask if she loved him, or to tell her how he felt. They knew all that already. Love had galloped through their lives bearing all before it. All that was left to them was this final decision.

She looked at him weakly, desiring to consent. He was so lovable, so warm, so gentle, so good to look at. There was no reason why she should hesitate.

Was there?

Yet she did hesitate, biting her lip, torn this way and that. Piero smiled at her, taking her hand, and her heart plunged with delight and love.

'Say yes,' he pleaded softly.

She heard her lips move, her tongue breathe the one word he wished to hear. His face lit up, he raised her hand to his lips and kissed it reverently.

That night, in her bed, she awoke from a deep but troubled sleep, the word No springing from her shaking lips.

She was damp with perspiration, shivering with fear. Cesare's dark face loomed in her mind, rage radiating from it.

'What have I done?' she asked herself weakly.

They flew to Milan. Amanda was surprised to realise, as she looked down at England's green fields, how little she regretted what she left behind. Despite what she had said to Piero, despite all she had told herself, she had never put down roots in England. The important, formative years had been spent elsewhere. She had secretly been an exile during these five years, an exile from the warm, sun-kissed plain of San Volenco. Now she was returning, and her heart was light.

She pushed away the night-time fears which her engagement had brought her. Why, as Piero said, should anyone be angry if she married him? Five years was long enough to wipe out all old debts.

They hired a car in Milan and set out to drive the rest of the way to Volenco.

According to the family legend, Volenco had been a knight during the first crusade who had returned to Italy unharmed, and on his journey home had seen a silvery stag leaping across the broad plain beyond a river. He had hunted it through the bright waters, across the plain and up the steep rocky fastness of a mountain, where it turned at last, its antlers forming a cross, before disappearing from his dazzled sight. Volenco had founded a monastery on the spot, convinced that he had seen a vision of Christ.

Over the years a settlement had grown up around the monastery walls. During the dangerous era of the early Middle Ages the Druetso family had somehow arrived, built their castle and surrounded both castle, town and monastery with battlemented walls which encircled the whole mountain. The monastery church, with its silver cross surmounting the ancient bell tower, still stood at the very summit, visible from miles away across the green plain. The Druetso had been driven out, during the Renaissance, to return again and re-take their old fortress in a bloody battle. One of the family had almost become Pope, only to die of a heart attack at a crucial moment. They had been soldiers, bankers, merchants, artists. Now they made their living in a timeless fashion from the soil—with vines and horses.

Dark portraits of them hung on the walls of the shadowy gallery above the hall—portraits which stretched back to the fifteenth century. The most famous was of Beatrice, a Botticelli, it was believed, although art historians disputed it. Beatrice di Druetso, a delicate ethereal girl with silvery fine, wayward hair and great pale blue eyes, a fine lustrous skin and a wistfully remote expression, was the subject of one of the city's most popular legends. Amanda, as a girl, had been told often that she resembled the portrait. She had spent hours staring at it, unable to believe she shared the fragile beauty of the subject.

As they drew nearer, Amanda was increasingly excited. Her mind opened to a rushing sense of the past. Memories possessed her, things she thought she had forgotten.

Fifteen miles away their car broke down. It was a sleepy, hot afternoon, and the nearest garage was closed for siesta. By the time the mechanic had been aroused, persuaded to look at their car and seen what was wrong, the dusk was fast falling around them. They went and sat on an old stone bridge, sipping fragrant local wine and sharing a pizza, savoury with anchovy, black olives and tomatoes. The mechanic sang in his tumbledown garage, clinking and clanking about in the entrails of the car. Children and dogs sidled up to inspect them, then ran away in mock alarm when they turned to grin.

'I'm so happy,' Amanda said suddenly. 'Darling, I'm afraid. What is waiting for us at Volenco? I've got ... a premonition ...'

Piero smoothed her cheek with a finger. 'Mm ... like a peach, your skin. Silly, silly *cara*. Afraid of what? Of those who love you? Mamma, Aunt Teresa, Giulio ...'

'Cesare,' she whispered huskily, her breath catching.

Piero's face darkened suddenly, in an uncharacteristic rage which reminded her of his brother. 'Cesare! Cesare!

Always Cesare! I begin to wonder how you really feel about that brother of mine!'

Amanda went white, then red. 'Piero! You're mad! You know I hate him. He frightens me.'

Piero's rage had already evaporated. He was too nice to be angry for long. He sighed and slid an arm around her waist. 'I know. I'm sorry. But don't worry. It will work out...'

When they arrived at the foot of the mountain road they could see that the city gates were locked, as they always were by ten o'clock. Against the dark sky the silver cross on the church gleamed brightly. The air was humid, heavy. Cars were not permitted inside San Volenco—the narrow, winding streets were too steep. They parked the car in the public car park, beneath a make-shift roof supported by wooden pillars, the nearest approach to a garage the city possessed. There were a dozen other vehicles parked there, among them a sleek silver Rolls, a vintage car which Amanda recognised as the possession of Cesare. Trust him to own something as exquisite and special as that! she thought crossly.

They walked slowly up the rough track leading towards the city gate. Suddenly the weather broke. Thunder crashed overhead, the osiers in the river bed tossed and rustled in the wind. Then the clouds poured down rain, filling the dry river bed with the rushing of water. Silver lightning split the darkness.

'Mother of God,' Piero shouted above the appalling din. 'What a welcome, my darling!'

They ran, panting, slipping, their feet unable to hold

on the rain-wet rock. Soaked, her thin cotton dress shrinking to her body, Amanda dived against the wall for some sort of protection while Piero furiously pulled the bell rope. The bell clanged noisily.

She looked at Piero and laughed, suddenly, half hysterical. 'You look so funny! Your shirt is saturated.'

The wicket gate opened. She turned, then her heart leapt into her throat.

'Cesare . . .'

Dark-visaged, unsmiling, a tall man in a white shirt open at the throat, his black hair slicked to his skull by rain, looking as menacing as some Renaissance prince confronting an enemy, Cesare let his narrow eyes survey her. She was wide-eyed, defiant, her fragility emphasised by her pallor and wind-tossed wet hair.

'She is soaked to the skin,' Piero protested, putting a quick, possessive arm around her.

The two men faced each other, and Amanda felt the confrontation as something physical. Piero's hand was clenched into a fist. She felt his arm tensing against her.

Then Cesare turned and silently led them into the city. They walked up the winding street to the castle. Faces peered out from windows above them, furtive and curious. Everyone knew they had arrived. Amanda felt the shuttered, inbred atmosphere of the old city closing around her once again. Now she remembered just how it felt, just what had always frightened her so much. In five years of England the impression had worn thin, but now it all came alive again—the menace of brooding possessiveness, the magic circle of the family. She was trapped in the web again, snared by the honey-sweet secretions love had used.

She shivered, and Cesare looked briefly down at her. 'Cold?' His voice sounded oddly familiar. Why did she remember those husky accents so well?

Piero was frightened, she suspected. He had not bargained for Cesare's silence, his coldness, his anger.

She looked up and saw the great wooden door of the hall open for them. A candle gleamed. She looked at Cesare. He felt her glance on him and turned again. 'The generator has just failed,' he said.

She laughed. 'Of course. It always does in storms.' It seemed almost a friendly act, a familiar and welcoming gesture. It reminded her of childhood games by candlelight in other storms, of her mother, comforting her with pancakes eaten picnic-style in bed, while beyond the windows the thunder cracked and the sky was riven by bright streaks of lightning.

'Amanda! *Cara!* Little one...' The Contessa hurried to the door, softly exclaiming her name again and again.

Amanda threw herself, half sobbing, into the arms which were extended to her, and was held warmly against a bony shoulder.

The Contessa's back was as straight, her widow's weeds as elegant and unchangeable as ever. She would wear black until the day she died. She had loved her husband passionately, and in her case the tradition of mourning was a true expression of grief.

Now she whispered gently, lovingly as she stroked Amanda's wet head, 'You are back at last where you belong. How could you stay away so long, *cara*? Here is your home, not England; the home of the family, the home of the heart . . .'

'I've missed you so much,' Amanda murmured, feeling the true depth of her affection for the Contessa Maria only now that she saw her again.

Cesare watched expressionlessly. Piero was kissing Aunt Teresa, assuring her that he had brought presents for the whole family. When the Contessa released her, Aunt Teresa bustled forward to embrace Amanda. Short, stout, with iron-grey hair which she wore in an ageless style, plaited across her head in a coronet, Aunt Teresa hugged Amanda warmly.

'But you are wet through! You must change! You will catch pneumonia if you stand about in these clothes.' Practical as ever, Aunt Teresa urged her towards the stairs. They climbed upwards into darkest shadow, curving at the top into a great gallery. Carrying a silver branched candelabrum of great age and beauty, Aunt Teresa led her up the stairs. The candlelight gradually ate the darkness, revealing fading tapestries, hung on the great stone walls, which billowed outward in the wind. Amanda gazed at them as she passed. They were as familiar to her as the faces of the family. There were the saints Agnes, Elizabeth and Veronica, their dim features softly visible among the shadows which had once been bright colours. The trees and leaves which had been green long ago were now a dusty sage. The flowers had softened and turned yellow. Here and there some member of the Druetso family had darned great rents in them.

They were still, for all their decay, exquisitely beautiful.

Amanda realised suddenly that Cesare had accompanied them. He was a step or two behind, his dark face implacable. She glanced back at him nervously.

Aunt Teresa paused before a door, opened it fumblingly, and Amanda gave a start as she realised which room she had been given.

'The Beatrice chamber!' she exclaimed. She had always slept in one of the smaller rooms when she stayed here.

Aunt Teresa looked nervously at Cesare. His grey eyes were watching Amanda. They gleamed with sardonic mockery. She saw it had been his decision to put her in this room, and she guessed why.

Beatrice, the girl in the Botticelli painting, had been betrothed to a Renaissance Druetso, an earlier Conte of San Volenco, and had fallen in love before their marriage with one of his own knights. Legend was ambiguous from that point on—one version of the story said that she married the Conte all the same, deserting her lover, and bore him three sons and a daughter. Another version, more popular and more dramatic, said that she leapt to her death from the balcony of this very chamber, down to the cruel valley below.

Amanda met Cesare's menacing look bravely. If he meant her to feel threatened he was wasting his time. Melodramatic legends did not impress her.

'You must have a bath and go to bed,' commanded Aunt Teresa. She lit a candle which stood ready on the bedside table, smiled at Amanda and left her.

Amanda found the small cupboard which had been turned into a bathroom during her time here, bathed and slid into one of her London nighties, a pale pink fantasy sewn with white rosebuds, sheer and fragile like a pink cloud.

Aunt Teresa eyed it reverently when she returned bearing a tray. 'Ah, *bellissima*! But is it warm enough? You forget, Amanda, how cold it is between these stone walls of ours at night?'

Amanda dived into her bed and smiled cheerfully at her. 'I'm as warm as toast!'

'Ah, what it is to have young blood,' sighed Aunt Teresa. She laid the tray on Amanda's knees. 'Soup. Hot rolls. Some nice spaghetti and coffee . . . now, eat it all, or you will get thinner and waste away before our eyes. So slim you are—but pretty! Prettier than a flower. How happy it would make your dear mother to see you like this and here again where you belong . . .'

Aunt Teresa had never married, had no children to spoil and dote upon, and so her life had been devoted to the adoration of her nephews and nieces. She had a bottomless well of love to give them. In return, she was perhaps the most loved member of the Druetso family. Italian family life retaining so much of the cohesive quality of family life in the past, an unmarried woman need not feel wasted—she was constantly needed, constantly valued for her contribution to the family.

When Amanda had eaten her meal, Aunt Teresa took the tray away, kissing her goodnight. 'Now, do not read

for too long! You have had a long journey. You need
sleep.'

Amanda read for a while, then obediently blew out her
candle. A few moments later she heard the rain stop. She
went out on to the balcony which ran outside her window
to stare out over the dark valley. The sky was still piled
high with dark storm clouds. The moon came out feebly,
shedding a pallid light.

Another balcony ran beneath her own. Suddenly a
match scraped. She smelt sulphur, saw the brief flare of
the flame. Unbearably curious, she peered over the rail to
see who had the room beneath. She had forgotten the
dispensation of rooms in the intervening years.

Cesare's face looked up at her. He was leaning on the
rail of his balcony, his cigarette in his hand, a wisp of
smoke curling up towards her. At this angle he had a
compressed strength of body, his features even more
darkly implacable.

They regarded each other in silence. She wondered if
he could hear the beating of her heart—it seemed to her
to be beating like a drum.

Then softly, chillingly, he said, 'Be careful, Amanda.
Remember the fate of Beatrice...' He looked down,
then up again, his lip curling. 'It is a long way down to
the valley.'

CHAPTER TWO

AMANDA had expected to sleep lightly, troubled on this first night back in San Volenco, but in fact her sleep was deep and dream-filled, and at dawn she was startled to be shaken awake by a gentle tapping on her bedroom door. Yawning, she sat up. 'Mmm?' She stared in disbelief at her bedside clock. Who could be waking her at such an hour?

'Come in,' she called, expecting to see Aunt Teresa with a cup of hot coffee. The door was pushed slowly open and Cesare leaned in the door frame. The heavy-lidded eyes scrutinised her.

Coming awake fast, she demanded, 'What is it? What do you want?'

For a moment he continued to regard her in mocking silence, surveying at his leisure her tumbled fair hair, her naked shoulders, the floating wisps of pink nylon which made such a vain attempt to clothe her. Her cheeks grew hot. She dived back under the bedclothes, pulling the sheet closer to her throat.

He laughed curtly. 'Have you forgotten I ride at first light? I've had Vesta saddled. I thought you might want to come along as you always used to do...'

'Vesta!' She had been given Volenco Vesta on her sixteenth birthday, and from the first there had been a deep affection between them. The pale, dappled grey

mare had a gentle, but teasing nature. She enjoyed playing tricks on her young owner, but was always easily
recalled to more serious business. Amanda had adored
her.

'Who has ridden her since I went away?' she asked
now, hoping that it had been someone who understood
Vesta's complex nature. It would be tragic if the mare's
soft mouth had been ruined by the jabbing of an unsym-
pathetic rider.

'Tina takes her out every morning,' Cesare told her.
He turned on his heel, his lean brown hand flicking a tan
leather crop against his breeches. 'I'll be in the stable
yard. I'll wait for five minutes.'

Amanda shot out of bed, forgetting her half-clothed
state, and ran after him. 'But what shall I wear? Jeans?'

He turned and let his cool eyes drift over her again.
'Your jodhpurs are in the chest,' he said shortly.

She was astonished. 'My old jodhpurs? They won't
still fit me, Cesare!'

'Nonsense,' he said. 'From the look of you I'd say you
haven't gained an inch in any direction. You were always
a skinny, underfed brat.'

He left the room and she opened the old-fashioned
chest which occupied one corner of the bedroom. The
jodhpurs were there, as he had said, neatly folded in
tissue paper and smelling faintly of lavender.

To her amusement they fitted her perfectly. She found
a white cotton polo-neck shirt, pushed it down into the
waistband of the jodhpurs and regarded herself in a full-
length, faintly spotted mirror which hung on the wall

facing the window. Suddenly she almost felt she was that eighteen-year-old girl who had last ridden Volenco Vesta over the plains below the walled city.

Giving her hair a last pat, she ran down into the stable yard, taking the back staircase by instinct, two steps at a time, just as she had always done. They were ancient, creaking wooden stairs, hollowed in the centre by the feet of generations. They led to the kitchens and thence to the stable.

The servants, of course, were already at work. Antonia was deftly rolling bread dough into torpedo-shaped rolls. Sandro was getting meat out of the freezer—new since her time, Amanda noted. These little changes struck her all the more vividly because so many things had stayed the same.

Giovetta was muttering as she prepared the breakfast, her gnarled hands deft and fast. She looked round and beamed. '*Buon giorno*, Amanda! So there you are.' Then she winked. 'He is waiting for you. Hurry. You know how it is with him if he is kept waiting! Ah, the tiger in him roars then!'

Amanda paused to kiss her withered cheek, smiled at Sandro and Antonia and fled onwards.

He was smoking a cigarette, staring away from her, his expression brooding. She stood watching him nervously. It was vital that Cesare should accept her marriage to his brother. Without his willing consent the family would be split into two. She could not contemplate being the cause of such division in the family. Somehow she had to persuade him to accept the marriage.

He turned and saw her. Something flared in the grey eyes. He dropped his cigarette and trod on it ruthlessly. 'Come along, then!' His voice was sharp.

They rode out under the stone arch surmounted by a stone stag caught in flight, with front feet poised. Following the winding road to the city gates they passed early risers who surreptitiously gazed at them, filled with intense interest but courteous enough to pretend otherwise. The gates were open to admit the morning supply of food from the plain; fruit, milk, eggs and vegetables sent from the flat fields which the river kept so well watered during the rainy season. During the height of the summer the river bed dried up, but centuries of irrigation had made the plains fertile. Today, after last night's rain, the banks were standing above muddy yellow water.

In the last years of the nineteenth century Cesare's great-grandfather had imported some English horses, six mares and a stallion, from which he had bred the famous Volenco strain which now sold for high prices, some of the horses even going back to England. Cesare bred them for speed and stamina, showing them at the increasingly popular Italian horse trials and shows. His dream, Amanda knew, was to take his horses to England some day and win the world-famous cups offered to international show-jumpers. Already the stables were papered with rosettes, and his offices held rows of silver cups and medals.

Today he was riding Volenco Viva, a tall black stallion with a thick, flowing mane and a rolling, arrogant eye which amused her by bearing a faint resemblance to Cesare's own expression.

She had grown up with these horses. She knew their pedigrees as well as he did, and had ridden with him from childhood. Her natural good seat and fearlessness had commanded his approval. Piero had disgraced himself at the age of six by crying and refusing to ride after a fall, but Amanda, although a baby of five when she had her first fall, had seemed unshaken by it. Looking back, she put this down to a lack of imagination rather than real courage. It had never entered her head that she might be seriously hurt when she took a fence. She had just followed doggedly in Cesare's wake, taking every fence that came, allowing her pony to use its own good sense if it wished to refuse anything it considered too high. She knew that her parents had often been anxious about her reckless riding, but Cesare had encouraged her, delighting in her skill and daring. When he gave her Volenco Vesta even the Contessa had been startled, since the mare was worth a fortune, being one of their best bred mares, but of course no one at San Volenco challenged a decision by the Conte.

Patting Vesta's sleek grey neck now, she said, 'Tina must be good with the horses. Vesta is as sensitive to touch as she ever used to be!'

'Tina's a good horsewoman,' he replied.

She shot him a teasing look, remembering Tina faintly, a peach-skinned creature three years her junior, with silky black hair and dark eyes, very much the Latin beauty. Was Cesare interested in her? Amanda wondered.

'Tina's very pretty, isn't she?' she asked.

He swivelled a cold grey eye. 'Very.'

Vesta began edging mischievously towards Viva, her tail flirting to and fro, making a snorting sound oddly reminiscent of laughter. Viva turned and showed his great teeth in a frightening gesture, and Vesta quickly dropped back and pretended meekness. Amanda laughed.

Cesare glanced at her enquiringly.

'Vesta is still the same naughty, teasing creature she always was!' she explained.

'She's a typical female,' said Cesare, his eyes charged with dry amusement.

The vineyards lay on their right now, the sun-dried pastures on their left. The horses were eager to stretch their legs in a gallop. Vesta strained at her bit, champing loudly.

'Let 'em go,' Cesare said suddenly.

Amanda dropped her hands and Vesta shot away in Viva's wake, her dainty neck arched, her mane flying out in the wind of her own motion.

The brightening sky was filled with an apricot light, filtered through palest misty gauze. Slowly blue was drifting across from the east and the apricot was fading. On the distant horizon lay the mountains, purple and mauve, mist-wreathed. They gave a meaning to the landscape which might otherwise have been dull.

San Volenco lay behind them. When they turned they

saw it rising from the plain like a backcloth to an early Renaissance painting, a layered wedding-cake with the church as its crest. The battlemented walls, the vista of roofs on many levels, the pastels of the walls of some houses, the Gothic architecture of the castle, all made of the city something strangely beautiful, a remnant of another time. The houses tumbled down the mountain-side in so haphazard a fashion that the eye was constantly surprised and enchanted, yet despite the wild variety of the place it had a unity born of time rather than style. Each age had added something without destroying what had been before, so that it had become welded into a whole.

Cesare reined in and sat back, waiting for her. His shirt lay open against his brown throat. His dark hair was whipped by the wind into attractive disarray.

'That was good,' he said with satisfaction. His eye approved her style as she joined him, riding easily, in perfect communion with her mare. 'You haven't lost your touch, I see. Ridden much in London?'

'I did some pony-trekking in Scotland last year,' she said.

'Fun?' he asked.

Amanda remembered the young man who had been her constant companion among the heather, and a reminiscent smile curved her lips. 'Great fun,' she said.

Cesare's brows quirked upwards. He looked hard at her. 'I see,' he drawled, his eyes coolly unreadable.

She was beginning to think that there was rather more to Cesare than she had realised at the tender age of eighteen. He had a way of saying things she found disconcerting, although she could not quite put her finger on what exactly it was she found so alarming.

Was it only that she found his mind baffling, always guarded, and that we tend to fear the unknown, preferring the devil we know to anything we do not understand? Or did her instinct warn her to beware of the autocratic master of San Volenco?

They rode back towards the city. Amanda was beginning to tire, although this had been an idyllic start to the day. There had been a tremendous sense of freedom when they were flying across the plain towards the blue haze of the mountains. She remembered many mornings when they had come back like this, silent and content.

They passed black-garbed women who raised sun-warmed faces to greet her. She smiled at them, remembered names, asked a few questions about families she had half-forgotten but which came hurrying back into her mind at the sight of these faces.

Cesare listened tolerantly as she was informed of the names of new *bambini*, the weddings performed, the deaths suffered.

As they rode on she said, 'How much has happened in five years!'

'You have an excellent memory,' he said, and managed to sound as if congratulating himself rather than her.

'They don't change,' she said.

He nodded. 'Comforting, isn't it?'

She looked startled. It was true, but again, how startling to have him say just what was in her own mind. He seemed to walk in and out of her thoughts as casually as he walked through the city. She found it disconcerting to have him so at home.

'Time has made little impact in San Volenco,' she said. 'Except that your mother does look older than I remember.'

He nodded. 'Your mother's death probably has more to do with that than the passage of time.'

'They were very close, weren't they?'

'Like sisters,' he agreed.

When they got back to the stables a girl was cleaning tack in the tackroom. She came out, a brass bit in her hand, her full lower lip pouting.

'Why is she riding my mare?' she demanded of Cesare.

Amanda swung down from Vesta's back, leaving Cesare to deal with the situation.

She had recognised Tina at once, of course. The girl was five years older, but still at the peak of her ripe beauty. She was wearing very tight blue jeans, her curvaceous figure excitingly emphasised by a lemon silk top which left nothing to the imagination. Her olive-skinned face had a sulky sensuality. She was Antonia's daughter and had always lived in the castle, brought up with the Contessa's children but never a member of the family, of course. As a girl she had been difficult and rebellious. Her earlier beauty had ripened, the golden bloom of sixteen departing as she matured.

'Vesta is Amanda's mare,' Cesare told her curtly. 'You know that.' He flung her his reins and swung down.

'Five years away, but she still owns her?' Tina asked sullenly.

'She is Amanda's,' Cesare repeated with a shrug. 'Take a look at Viva's right rear hock. A touch of his old trouble, I'm afraid.'

Amanda was horrified by this autocratic behaviour. She gave Tina a worried, apologetic smile and turned to speak to Cesare, but he was already stalking into the castle. He turned and snapped his fingers at her. 'Come along!' The tone was peremptory. Seething, she ran after him.

This was how she remembered him—dictatorial, domineering, a domestic tyrant!

It was natural that Tina should resent Amanda's resumption of ownership of Vesta. For five years she had no doubt ridden the mare and regarded her as her own. Now the mare was suddenly taken away from her, and Tina expected to put up with a fait accompli.

When she caught up with Cesare's dark, striding figure she demanded hotly, 'Did you have to be so beastly to Tina?'

'Tina is my stable girl. She should have learnt by now to hold her tongue and do as she is bid,' he snapped.

'I don't blame her for being upset,' Amanda began again.

'You know nothing about it,' he said. 'Be quiet.'

She gasped in outrage. How dared he speak to her like that? He was ahead of her again, walking with that graceful lope, like some wild animal stalking through a dark jungle, his black head held high, tilting as he

glanced upward. The Counts of Volenco had all been
cast in the same mould. The gloomy portraits hanging in
the gallery made that plain. Broad-shouldered, lean, with
hard, fit bodies, they had dominated their landscape as
they did the paintings. They hung in a row; the same
dark, arrogant, handsome features looking out of one
canvas after another, lips lifted in a sneer, eyes insolently
sure of themselves; predatory, commanding, confident.

He paused and she opened her mouth to begin the
argument again, but he spoke first.

'You must be hungry. Wash your hands and we'll go
to breakfast.'

His suggestion was perfectly reasonable, but why did
he have to deliver it in that commanding voice, sure that
obedience must follow? It made one long to disobey,
however foolishly. Even the meekest soul, thought
Amanda, must long to rebel.

Breakfast was served as it had always been in a small,
bright room overlooking a garden. Pots of geraniums
stood along the windowsill, their scarlet flowers brilliant
above the terracotta clay. The sun streamed in past and
over them, filling the bright air with golden dust.

The walls were painted white. The floorboards had the
shining patina of great age. The family were seated
around a long, highly polished refectory table. A pot of
basil stood in the centre, the traditional method of keeping away flies. A yellow enamelled bowl of fruit was
reflected in the table surface. They came in together,
Cesare slightly behind Amanda, and the family looked
round at them.

Contessa Maria lifted her smooth cheek for a morning kiss, her face filled with content. Amanda felt a qualm as she saw that look.

'You have enjoyed your ride?'

Amanda rested her cheek on top of the dark head. 'It was marvellous! I'd forgotten how good it felt to get up early in the morning and go for a ride. The air smells sweeter and the world seems much more beautiful. Now I'm starving—I could eat a horse!'

'A horse?' Contessa Maria looked startled, then laughed. 'Oh, the English joke! So long since we heard them! Sit, my love. The rolls are still warm, and Giovetta has sent up your favourite cherry jam, her best ever. This year you will be here again to help her make it, that will make her very happy. Every year she has sighed over your absence when she made the cherry jam. It reminded her of you.'

Piero rose and drew out a chair, but Cesare, ignoring him, firmly seated Amanda beside himself.

Piero flushed dark red, and everyone else stared at their plates. Amanda was dumb with confused embarrassment. She gave Piero an anxious, placatory smile, pleading with him to understand why she did not quarrel with his brother.

Cesare offered her the basket of rolls, wrapped in their white damask napkin.

She took one, her gaze reproachful. He returned her look blandly. 'Jam? Butter?'

She accepted both and began to eat. Cesare poured her coffee, thick and fragrant, from the huge silver pot standing in the middle of the table. A family heirloom, it was battered, polished lovingly until the fine engraving was almost invisible, and in daily use. Nothing here was just for show.

The family resumed their own meal. Piero stirred his coffee and drank it, watching his brother over the rim of his cup. Two spots of red burnt in the centres of his cheeks.

Suddenly he said, 'Amanda and I would like to be married this summer.'

A silence followed the throwing down of this gauntlet. Cesare bit into a roll. He stirred his coffee too, his eyes fixed on his spoon. Everyone sat like statues waiting for him to react, watching which way the cat would jump.

'Piero is in no position to get married,' he said at last, in a calm voice addressed pointedly to Amanda. 'He has not yet established himself, I'm afraid.'

Amanda looked at Piero. He was staring fixedly at his brother, his eyes narrowed. He stuttered when he replied, his control over his temper slipping badly, 'I—I'm the best p-p-person to judge that, I think. If I want to get m-married, I will, and no one can stop m-m-me.'

Cesare laughed.

The sound was like a whip flicked across Piero's face. It made him turn white and shake. The contempt was unbearable. After a moment he stood up, his chair grating across the floor.

Cesare lifted his grey eyes, then, and looked coolly at his brother. 'Sit down.'

Piero stood his ground. 'You can't give me orders in

that tone of voice, Cesare. I am a grown man now. Amanda loves me and she is going to be my wife.'

There was another silence, charged with electricity. Contessa Maria looked from one to the other of her sons in pain, biting her lip.

Cesare stared at Piero. 'Is this a place for such a discussion?'

'Things must be settled,' Piero insisted. He was looking calmer now. He had lost the stutter and looked less vulnerable to Cesare's biting scorn.

'Well, well. well,' drawled the elder brother. 'So this is what it takes to turn the young calf into a bull?' He sounded amused. His grey eyes measured Piero and received a challenge in return.

The tension around the table noticeably lessened. The Contessa released her held breath in a sigh.

'Sit down, Piero. You can't shout at me like this at my own breakfast table,' said Cesare lightly.

Reluctantly, Piero sat. Amanda lifted the silver pot, wincing at its unremembered weight, and poured him another cup of coffee, pushing it towards him with a smile which soothed. Cesare watched this by-play with a little smile of his own. Catching it, she was not sure she liked it.

'I have to get down to the vineyard to see Sponelli,' Cesare said, finishing his own coffee with a gulp. '*Ciao*, Mamma ... better start thinking about wedding clothes, eh? That will give you something to be cheerful about!'

He had backed down! Amanda stared at the closed door. Cesare had actually permitted Piero to challenge

him and had left the field to his brother! It was so unbelievable that she looked round the table to see if she
had imagined it.

She saw a dazed expression on everyone's face. Even
Piero looked warily incredulous. It was the first time, she
suspected, that he had ever won an argument with his
brother—Cesare was not inclined to permit opposition to
his will. His autocratic nature forbade it. He was accustomed to commanding and receiving obedience.

Contessa Maria was looking sad, and Amanda noticed
it with regret. She felt guilty. After all, she had already
been responsible for inflicting a hurt upon the Contessa
when she refused Cesare. Now she had compounded her
injury by getting engaged to Piero. Her guilt was all the
more powerful because the relationship between them
had always been so close. There is an affection which
bypasses blood ties. Because of the love the Contessa had
felt towards Amanda's mother, Amanda had always
regarded the Contessa as a second mother.

She gently laid her hand over the Contessa's fingers. 'I
am sorry that my return has caused trouble.'

'Not your return, dear child. We are all happy to see
you back in San Volenco.'

'It is our engagement,' Piero said.

The Contessa flinched from the brutal statement. She
sighed, her thin shoulders lifted in a Latin gesture of
regret. Amanda smiled at her.

'Cesare will come round,' she comforted.

The Contessa looked doubtful. 'It is his pride, the
pride of the Druetso. It is unbending.'

'After five years surely he can't still resent my refusal!'
Amanda murmured.

'Five years or fifty years! Time is meaningless in such
a case,' said the Contessa.

'Piero and I...' began Amanda.

'Must be patient,' the Contessa finished for her.

Castle and city were knit into one unit by the family—
most of the people of San Volenco were, however re-
motely, connected by marriage. Much inbreeding had
gone on here in past centuries. It was only recently that
outsiders had been accepted. The spread of air travel, the
arrival of tourism and the change in living conditions
generally had begun to alter the concept of life as the
people saw it, nevertheless they had managed so far to
hang on to their closed-ranks attitudes.

The motto of the city was carved in stone above the
ancient gates. As a child Amanda had often gazed up at
the Latin words and marvelled at them. Cesare had
translated them for her in his deeply serious voice. 'In
life, fidelity. In death, fidelity.' Then he had asked her,
'Can you understand what that means, Amanda?'

She had frowned, reaching for the concept, as serious
as himself for all her youth. 'I think so, Cesare. We must
be faithful in life or death?'

He had searched her smooth-skinned little face with
those cold grey eyes of his, then nodded with satisfaction.

So that as Amanda walked through the narrow, winding streets that afternoon, with Piero, she was not surprised by the reserve she met with, the holding back which

she recognised where a stranger might have been fooled by their affectionate smiles. Their disapproval was so subtly expressed. The smiles never quite reached those dark, watchful eyes, and their greetings were ambiguous, shaded from courtesy to downright disapproval. The people felt that Amanda was betraying the Conte. They knew, as did everyone in the city, that Cesare had once asked her to marry him. They knew the long-cherished dreams of the Contessa and Amanda's mother. In the eyes of the city Amanda was betrothed to Cesare and therefore could never belong to his brother Piero.

How could she, in these circumstances, fail to feel extremely uncomfortable? She could not even protest that her refusal of Cesare ended the matter, for she knew very well that these people knew their Conte better. He had never brooked opposition to his will in the past. Why should he permit a chit of a girl to defy him now?

When they returned to the castle Piero led her into the walled garden which lay within the building, a small enclosure built into an angle of the crenellated wall looking out over the valley. A few box trees made a pleasant shade in which the women of the household often came to sit with their sewing. Long stone troughs contained geraniums, pansies and carnations, petunias and other gaily coloured flowers. Creepers insinuated themselves along the walls, softening the starkness of the stone and encouraging birds to perch and sing among their leaves.

Piero pulled her close. 'It seems like a hundred years since we were alone.'

'Piero, did you get the feeling that we're unpopular out

there?' Amanda tried to laugh, but it was difficult. 'There were icy fingers running up and down my spine everywhere we walked. If looks were daggers I would lie out there on the cobblestones as cold as charity.'

Her colloquial English had evaded him. He frowned down at her. 'What do you mean? I do not understand.'

She reverted to Italian. 'They hate me.'

'I should have married you in England,' he said shakily, without denying her accusation.

'We couldn't!' Amanda's emancipation in England had not gone so far as to allow her to consider such an affront to the family. She looked up at him sombrely. 'They would never have forgiven that.'

Piero looked desperate. 'What are we going to do, *cara mia*? Cesare's face when we arrived! I never suspected.' He caught back his breath, then released it with a shrug. 'Had he struck me he could not have astonished me more! I thought he had forgotten you, that he had only proposed out of family duty and perhaps even been relieved when you turned him down. He has barely mentioned your name since you left.' He looked down, his narrowed eyes probing hers. 'Amanda, tell me the truth now. Does Cesare love you?'

'No, no!' She recoiled, going first scarlet, then white, her breath suddenly hurting in her lungs. 'Of course not! You were right to call it a matter of family duty. You know our mothers always wished it, talked of it as something expected. It came as a bolt out of the blue to me. I was too young to listen to them, but afterwards I realised they had always planned it.'

'Then why is he so angry?' Piero asked unanswerably.

'Perhaps it is as your mother said—pride, Druetso pride. Cesare was always an arrogant, unbending brute. I wounded his pride when I refused him, now I've re-opened the injury by coming back engaged to you.'

'It is strange that you never loved him,' Piero said thoughtfully. 'Half the girls in the city fell for Cesare at one time or another.'

'I suppose I saw him as a tyrannical older brother,' she shrugged. 'I was half English, remember. I didn't want to marry without love. I needed my independence.'

Piero caught her closer, kissing her with a hungry desperation. 'You shall not marry without love, I promise you. Cesare shall not separate us. The city shall not come between us.'

Amanda clung to him, feeling his warmth enclosing her as the ancient, sun-kissed walls enclosed the garden.

Suddenly a crash exploded beside them. They leapt apart, too badly shaken to realise what had happened for a moment. When they saw and heard normally again Amanda's brain flinched at the realisation of what had happened. A shattered terracotta flowerpot lay beside them on the path. Earth and leaves, a mangled red flower like a splash of blood, lay scattered in a semi-circle. Her widening eyes slowly rose. Along the balcony of Cesare's room stood a row of terracotta flowerpots. There was a glaring gap in their ranks.

'Did it fall or was it pushed?' she asked on a stifled, half-hysterical giggle.

'God, he might have killed us!' Piero was very pale.

Amanda could not stop laughing. 'Apparently Cesare is even angrier than we had begun to suspect,' she said. Then she shuddered, covering her face with her hands in a wave of icy misery. 'Oh, Piero! What are we to do?'

CHAPTER THREE

Two days later, Piero returned to work in the family wine business. There was no question of a holiday for him, Cesare made that clear, and Piero explained to Amanda that he thought it best not to argue with his brother on the point.

'We will still see plenty of each other in the evening and at weekends,' he assured her.

'What shall I do during the day, though? I must have something to occupy me or I shall go mad. I'm not accustomed to idleness.'

'You're on holiday!'

'I'm no tourist,' she pointed out.

'Help my mother, then,' Piero suggested, his mind only partly on their conversation; he was tracing the line from temple to throat, his lips silkily caressing as he brushed them along cheek, ear, throat.

She laughed, but pushed him away. 'No, listen to me! Seriously, Piero, I must do something! You've no conception how boring it can be to be at a loose end.'

'But, *cara*, there is so much to do in the house. The women work from dawn to dusk. There will be something for you to do.'

Amanda bit her lip. She did not quite like the way he equated women with housework. Still, she was quite

45

ready to help in the house, if help was needed, so she dropped the subject.

'Where will we live when we are married?' she asked casually. It had occurred to her that they might live in one of the town houses, the sort which tumbled down the narrow alleys towards the walls, their roofs crooked and weathered with time, painted pink or white, their small windows brightened by a window-box of geraniums. It would be fun, like living in a dolls' house.

Piero shrugged. 'Why, here, of course.'

'In the castle?' She looked at him incredulously. 'Oh, no, Piero!'

'But of course in the castle—where else?'

'I want a home of my own,' she protested.

'But this is my home, and when we have the babies my mother will be always at hand to help you with them. How happy that will make her! You know how she loves you, and how she will adore our children when they arrive!' His dark eyes reflected a bewildered hurt. 'Why do you look so cross? I thought you loved Mamma...'

'Of course I do! I always have! And it will be wonderful to have her to help and advise me!' She looked anxiously at him. 'But still, Piero, I think we should have our own home. Independence, privacy, the chance to make your own decisions—a home of your own gives you all those. Don't you see? We are always surrounded by people here in the castle. There are eyes and ears in the very walls. I feel as if I'm in a goldfish bowl. We're never really alone.' She clutched at him, laying her head on his shoulder, and whispered, 'Piero, it frightens me...'

'Frightens you? What does, darling?' Piero looked quite bewildered.

'Don't you see? Haven't you noticed? No one here takes our engagement seriously. They shrug it off, ignore its very existence. I think they're waiting for us to ... oh, I'm not sure how to put it, how to describe it ... they're waiting for us to come to our senses, I suppose!'

Piero's face darkened. 'Yes,' he admitted heavily, 'I've felt that, too. But they will come round!'

'No,' she cried. 'They treat us with kindly tolerance, as if we're lunatics. They're sure it will never happen!'

'Then we must show them how wrong they are!'

She moved away, shivering. 'It's Cesare! They've taken their cue from him. He takes this attitude, so they all follow suit. They believe...' Her voice cut off, she went white.

Piero stared down at her. 'What do they believe?' Then, intuitively catching her meaning, he caught her back against him, holding her with hungry determination. 'Don't look like that. He shan't have you. You're mine now.' Then, on a fierce note, 'I would kill you first!'

She laughed. 'I'm not sure I find that such a comforting prospect, but I love you, Piero...'

They kissed lingeringly, leaning together like children looking for comfort.

Amanda wandered along to the kitchen later, to beg for a chance to be useful. Giovetta was making a great pan full of risotto, her face intent upon her task.

'Can I do anything?' Amanda asked her. 'I'm at a loose end. I'd love to do a useful job of work.'

'No, no,' clicked Giovetta reprovingly. 'Enjoy yourself while you're young. Sunbathe in the garden, go for a walk, listen to the transistor, eh? Life's too short.' Then she gave a sharp glance at Sandro who, his feet propped up on the table, was snoring beneath a large red handkerchief. 'Eh, lazy good-for-nothing, do some work for a change! Wake up ... *basta*! Get on with your job, you ...'

Amanda wandered out disconsolately. She went in search of her aunt and found her in the bedrooms, checking a laundry list. 'Help me? Do I look as if I need help? You're on holiday, child. Go for a walk in the town. Look up old friends. Go for a ride ... Cesare will find you a mount!'

'I rode this morning,' Amanda said.

The Contessa looked at her sharply. 'Of course, with Cesare! Well, amuse yourself, my dear.'

'I'm bored,' Amanda sighed.

'Ah, the modern disease!' The Contessa disapproved of her. 'When I was young we were never bored. We were either working so hard we had no time to be so, or we were enjoying ourselves.'

'I want to work hard,' Amanda pointed out. 'Piero has gone back to work and Giovetta won't have me in the kitchen. Do let me help you, Contessa?'

The Contessa considered her. 'I know! You can take a parcel down to Giulio for me.'

Giulio had bought the antique shop when Amanda's father sold it. He had totally changed the business in the years since he took over. He had cut down on the number of genuine antiques he sold, and now specialised in reproductions, without bothering to distinguish too clearly between what was genuine and what was a modern copy. Amanda had seen several items in his window which she had recognised as reproductions, which were not labelled as such, but which were priced far beyond their true value. She suspected that Giulio had never stepped beyond the legal line. No doubt, if pressed, he would admit that an object was a copy, but many customers probably bought without enquiring as to authenticity. They were quite as happy with fakes so long as the brutal truth was not pushed down their throats.

The shop was housed in a medieval house of great charm, the ground floor having been turned into a bay-windowed display room, so elegantly laid out now that customers could wander through the shop and get the impression that they were actually in a private home, although the objects were all for sale. No prices were displayed inside the shop. Only the objects actually seen in the window were priced—and these were generally the cheaper items.

Amanda paused to gaze through the window. A polished spinning wheel, a copper vase and a small octagonal table were the only objects on display today. They were all reproductions and all highly priced in the circumstances, but she had to admit that they looked very attractive. Giulio had a gift for such displays.

Giulio came from the back of the shop to greet her with every sign of delight, yet somehow she sensed that her arrival was inopportune. Even as he kissed her hand with Italianate gallantry he flickered a nervous glance towards the narrow stairs which wound upwards from one side of the room. Amanda was sure she heard someone moving about up there.

As with most of the people in the city, Giulio had vague family connections with the castle. Amanda had known him all her life. His family ran the biggest hotel in the city. A slim, olive-skinned young man, he had greenish eyes, rare in the family, and the usual dark hair.

'The Contess sent me to deliver this parcel,' Amanda said, handing him her burden.

'Ah! At last! She has promised to let me sell this for so long that I was beginning to believe she would never part from it!' He carefully unwrapped a large glass bowl which Amanda recognised with dismay as one of the family heirlooms. Were the Druetso family so much in need of money that they had to sell their treasured possessions?

Giulio set it on a long refectory table, fussed over it, moving it here and there, until he was satisfied. 'There ... that looks great, eh?'

'Giulio, why is the Contessa selling it?' Amanda asked tentatively.

He shrugged. 'It was part of her dowry. It is hers, not the property of the Conte. If she wishes to sell, that is her affair.'

Suddenly feet clattered down the wooden stairs and

Tina appeared. For once she was not wearing her jeans, but a rather stunning gypsy-style dress made of vivid yellow silk, with a tight waist and a low, curved neckline which left most of her sun-gilded bosom exposed. She looked sensually inviting. From the fullness and gloss of her moist lips Amanda suspected she had recently been very thoroughly kissed, and she glanced curiously at Giulio.

He was frowning, his cheeks rather red. 'Ah, Tina,' he stammered. 'K-kind of you to do my housework for me...'

Tina had stopped dead at the sight of Amanda. She ignored Giulio but burst out suddenly, 'What are you doing here? Spying on me? Well, miss, two can play at that game! I would have thought you had enough trouble without asking for more!'

'Be quiet, Tina,' Giulio said hurriedly.

She ignored him, jerking her pretty shoulder away in a gesture that made him scowl. 'Do you know, English girl, what we did with spies not so long ago? We poured boiling oil into their ears and down their treacherous throats to teach them a lesson!'

Amanda could not help it—she burst out laughing. The threat was so absurdly melodramatic.

Tina looked furious. She loathed being laughed at. Putting her hands on her slender hips in a virago manner, she scornfully flicked her eye over Amanda. 'I don't know what they see in you, the Druetso men! You're not even particularly pretty!'

Giulio grabbed her by the arm, her flesh showing

white where his grip held. 'Stop it, do you hear? Are you mad to talk to her like this?'

'I'm not afraid to speak my mind!'

'She will be the Conte's sister-in-law, stupid girl!'

'I do not forget what the Conte said when Piero wrote to tell him that he wished to marry her! To his own mother the Conte said it—never while there is breath in my body, he said. I would sooner see my brother dead at my feet.' Tina's eyes flashed at Amanda as she repeated the words. 'This English girl will never marry Piero. The Conte has said it.'

Amanda turned on her heel and walked out, refusing to listen as Giulio pursued her, babbling apologies. Tears stung at the back of her eyes.

Even if she discounted some of what Tina had said as pure malice, she knew that the grain of truth which was left was disastrous. Cesare was popular. No wonder the people watched her and Piero with wary disbelief. They all knew from the gossip that Cesare was against the marriage, that he had sworn never to permit it.

Without being aware of her surroundings she returned to the castle, meeting no one on her way, and slipped into the little walled garden, sitting down on a stone bench beneath the droop of dusty ivy, hearing the birds sing and watching the shadow of wings on the pavement.

Her eyes felt heavy. The sunlight lay warmly on her face. She had a sudden longing to be back in England, safe from this tangled web in which she was trapped.

Somehow she had to persuade Cesare to change his mind. She knew it would not be easy; he was proud and unyielding. But there must be a way.

Later, crossing the great hall, she met Cesare himself, and almost laughed aloud at her own wild imagination. She had been sitting in the garden racking her brains to think of a way of coaxing Cesare to relent and here he was in the flesh—so little the ogre she had begun to think him in her private nightmares that she was almost weak with relief.

He was grubby, untidy, his dark hair falling in a tumbled mass over a face smeared with earth and green stains from the vines he had been tending.

He passed her with a silent nod, his expression abstracted, but on an impulse she stopped him, her hand touching his elbow. 'Cesare, could I have a word with you?'

He looked surprised, as if he had hardly noticed who it was. 'What, now? I must wash . . .' And he extended his hands for her to see the stains on them. 'Is it urgent?'

'Not urgent, but if you have any spare time . . .' She sounded sweetly submissive.

He gave her a suspicious look. 'Hmm . . . In my office in ten minutes, then.'

Amanda watched his departing back with triumph. She had just had an idea. Before she left for England she had done some translation work down at the vineyard offices. If Cesare allowed her to do so again, she would be working with Piero all day.

He had an office in the angle of one of the towers. He spent part of every day there, doing the estate work, making telephone calls and writing letters to all parts of the world. Several times a week one of the local women came in to do some secretarial work for him.

The office was bright, stark, modern. The sun filtered in through a venetian blind and made golden patterns on the polished floor. The only furniture was a desk and chair, a metal filing cabinet and a few bookshelves. Amanda ran a hand along the books. Accountancy. Wine making. Horses. They were all practical works, books of reference rather than books which revealed the personality of the owner.

She sat down in the revolving chair behind the desk and spun it with her feet, revolving cheerfully.

'What a child you are,' said his voice at the door.

She laughed at him over her shoulder and a queer feeling of *déjà vu* came over her which she later traced to the memory of seeing Piero as she rode the merry-go-round on Hampstead Heath. Inverted like this, their faces were oddly similar, and she was aware of the same curious, troubling sensation of pleasure in the sight of him.

He came across the room softly and put a hand on the chair to halt its progress, standing over her in a manner which made her hackles rise.

'Out of there!'

'The master's chair?' she retorted, teasing him.

'Yes,' he returned blankly.

She took her time in moving, but he did not give her the satisfaction of rising to her coat-trailing. He took the seat she had abdicated, watching her as she crossly sat down on the window-sill. Deep-silled, in a wide stone bay, the window looked out upon the sunlit city. Amanda could see the stalls in the market place, hear the cries of the vendors as they hailed passing tourists.

Cesare leant his elbows on the desk, his head lowered between his hands, and stared at her expressionlessly.

'So?'

'I want a job,' she said.

His brows jerked together. For a moment he did not speak. The grey eyes surveyed her thoughtfully. She wondered what he was thinking, and knew she would never be able to guess. Unknowable, immovable Cesare! An alien continent, distant and incredible, for ever locked against her probing mind.

At last he said slowly, 'You want a job? So being Piero's wife is not enough for you?'

'I'm not his wife yet.'

His mouth curled in an infuriating smile. 'True,' he murmured, and she did not like the way he said it.

'Although of course I soon shall be,' she added forcefully, in case he mistook her meaning.

'No need to shout,' he replied in maddening uncon-cern. 'Or glare defiance.'

She went pink and looked at him with dislike. He had used an old trick, allowing her own attack to defeat her. She felt foolish.

'Well,' he demanded lazily, 'what sort of job?'

'I thought you might need some translation done,' she said quickly. 'I did that before, remember.'

'I remember,' he said. 'Right—report to me at nine o'clock tomorrow.'

'At the vineyard?' she asked eagerly.

'Here,' he said.

'Oh, but I thought...' She was aghast. She had always worked in the office down at the vineyard itself. The vineyard and the stables were separate business ventures. The work Cesare did up here in the castle was much wider, more connected with San Volenco itself than with the day-to-day running of his two businesses.

'I have a translator already,' he said abruptly. 'But as it happens I'm organising a pageant to celebrate the Beatrice portrait. It is five hundred years old—we have only just realised how old it is. We were so used to it here. But an art expert who came here some weeks ago pointed out to me how valuable it is and it occurred to me that we should do something to celebrate it. I shall need more help, so your offer is timely.'

Amanda opened her mouth to protest. Her idea had been to spend each day near Piero, and the thought of spending them, instead, so close to Cesare was a terrifying one. Yet how could she refuse? He had been helpful, he had responded practically to her demand for work. How could she now refuse to do as he asked?

Before she had sorted out her chaotic thoughts the telephone rang. Cesare picked it up and answered, then his voice dropped intimately. 'Ah, *cara*! It is you. I hoped you would ring.' He covered the receiver with one hand and glanced at Amanda coolly. 'That was all you wanted? Then I'll see you at nine tomorrow.'

She was dismissed courteously. Flushed and feeling like a schoolgirl leaving the headmaster's study, she left the room. Behind her his voice spoke in mellifluous Italian, charm in every syllable. Who was on the receiving end of the honeyed talk? she wondered.

Before dinner that evening she had a chance to talk to Piero alone. He came hurrying to meet her, freshly showered, fragrant with after shave, his dark eyes eager.

'*Cara mia*, I've been looking forward to this all day ...' He reached for her and she melted into his arms.

As he drew back from the long kiss, he sighed. 'Was it worth waiting for?'

'What do you think, Piero?' She hugged him. 'It has been a very long day, though.'

'For me, too, angel! My mind was not on my work. Half a dozen times Cesare roared at me like a lion.'

Cesare ... The name dampened her spirits. She drew a deep breath. 'Piero, did you know Cesare is organising some sort of celebration for the five hundredth year since the Beatrice was painted?'

Piero looked bored. 'There has been talk of it.'

'He ... he wants me to help him organise it,' she said nervously. 'I'm not sure what sort of work it will be. Translating letters of one kind or another, I suppose.'

A frown darkened the boyish face. 'What? Did he ask you to do this? He can pay someone! My wife-to-be is not his servant!'

Hurriedly she explained. 'No, you see, I asked him if I could work down at the vineyard, to be near you, you understand. I meant I would do some translating down there. We could see each other more often, then.'

Piero kissed her. 'Little foolish girl ...'

'Unfortunately Cesare misunderstood. He ... offered me this other job, at the castle, working for him.' Her voice faltered. 'I didn't like to refuse—I was afraid I would offend him. I would hate to cause trouble in the family.'

Piero gazed thoughtfully at her. 'I see what you mean, of course, and you are quite right. If you help Cesare with this project of his it may soften him. He will be grateful. He will forget his anger.' He became suddenly enthusiastic, his dark eyes dancing. 'Yes, yes, I am sure it will alter his attitudes. Cesare loves the Beatrice portrait more than anything else the family owns. That is why he is organising this pageant of celebration. Nothing else could touch him as this will do.'

The family heard the news at dinner. The Contessa looked sharply at her eldest son, frowned, but was silent for a moment. Aunt Teresa was cheerfully delighted. She would welcome anything she took to be a sign of Cesare's relenting towards Piero and Amanda. After a while the Contessa said quietly, 'It will be good for Amanda to be busy, perhaps.' But her eyes were anxious as they rested on Cesare.

Tina was not at dinner with the family, but Amanda passed her that evening on the stairs, and the girl gave her an insolent look. 'So you are to be alone with the Conte all day, eh? Going to London has taught you a few tricks.'

Amanda ignored her. She was learning how to deal with the other girl's spite. Rising to the bait was fatal; it was best to ignore her darts.

Aunt Teresa, however, was more vulnerable. Somehow or other Tina managed to arouse the older woman's anxiety. Next morning she followed Amanda upstairs to the office, gently murmuring, 'I have been thinking ... perhaps unwise for you ... Tina says such things ... not that anyone would believe them! But your poor mother! Ah, what would she say, how would she advise you? Do you really think you should do this, dearest child? Not that Cesare ... no, he would not, I am sure! Head of the family betray the trust in him? I said to that bad girl, no, Tina ...'

At the door of Cesare's office Amanda turned and took Aunt Teresa's face in her two hands, kissing her firmly on her small nose, the nose which looked so oddly comic in the centre of that sun-baked old face. 'Darling Aunt, stop clucking like an old hen! Cesare is not an ogre, and I am not Snow White ...'

Aunt Teresa looked baffled. 'Eh?'

Cesare flung open the door. 'What is going on?'

Aunt Teresa squawked, unhappily, and fled.

Cesare grinned wickedly at Amanda. 'You have confused her, with your ogres and Snow Whites ...'

'You were eavesdropping!'

'This is my office, remember! How could I help overhearing that very audible conversation?'

She flushed and went into the room. A small table and chair had appeared in it since her last visit. On the table lay a pile of letters. 'These are all to be answered. You type, don't you?'

'Of course,' she nodded. 'But first ... Cesare ...'

'Yes?' His voice was bland.

'I think that the fact that I'm working for you may cause some gossip,' she began unhappily.

'No!' There was a distinct twinkle in the grey eyes.

She ground her teeth together. He was making fun of her. 'I got that impression from Aunt Teresa just now ...'

'So I heard,' he murmured, tongue in cheek.

'And from ... others,' she added frostily.

'Others?' He raised a polite brow.

She flushed. She would not mention Tina. 'Yes,' she said hastily passing on, 'others, and I thought perhaps we ought to forget about it. I mean, of course I would have liked to do the work, but in the circumstances ...'

'What circumstances?'

'Why, the gossip,' she mumbled, taken aback. 'We don't want to cause gossip, do we?'

'People will gossip whatever we do,' he shrugged. 'I've always found the best policy is to ignore other people and just carry on doing what I want to do, regardless.'

'Oh!' She was dumbfounded. It cut the ground from under her feet. She thought rapidly, then said, 'Oh, well, perhaps it would be a good idea if you made it clear that I'm working for you because you approve of my marriage to Piero ...'

'But I don't,' he said softly.

She went white, then red.

'I don't approve at all,' he added. 'And I never will.'

'Why can't you just pretend to them all?' she begged.

'Why should I? You would make Piero a disastrous wife.'

Her mouth dropped open incredulously. 'What?'

Cesare laughed, leaning back in his chair, his hands in his pockets. 'If you could see your face! I wish I had a camera!'

'What do you mean?' she demanded angrily.

'I thought I'd made myself tolerably clear. Your Italian is usually so fluent, too.' He sounded pleased with himself.

Stamping her foot in a childish fit of rage, she demanded again, 'Why would I make a disastrous wife? I love Piero and he loves me.'

'Piero would be putty in your pretty little hands,' Cesare said coolly. 'He is far too pliable for a spirited creature like you. Inside a year you would be running the marriage and you would both be desperately unhappy. Piero must be master in his own house—he is an Italian, it is necessary to his pride. It would be fatal for him to have a wife who was stronger than himself.'

'I love him. There would never be a question of dominance between us. We would be partners.'

'How little you know yourself,' Cesare murmured. He stood up and took two strides towards her. Amanda began to back instinctively, but he had seized her wrist in a firm grip. He looked down at her with lazy amusement. 'Steel to the core, Amanda. You neither bend nor break, do you?'

'Let me go!'

'Suppose I will not let you go?'

Her breath caught and she looked at him furiously. 'You would force me to be undignified,' she told him.

He laughed, throwing back his head in rich amusement.

She kicked him hard on the ankle and he stopped laughing.

'Vixen!' He released her, hopping on one foot.

Amanda moved to the far side of the room. 'If you come near me again I'll hit you with something!'

He threw up his hands in a gesture of submission. 'Pax! Get on with the letters. I'm going down to the stables.'

When he had gone she sat down with a thump and stared at the door. 'This isn't going to work,' she told herself aloud. 'I don't trust that man.'

CHAPTER FOUR

THE idea of the Beatrice pageant seemed to capture the imagination of many organisations. Amanda soon found herself swamped with work, answering letters and telephone queries; ordering costumes, suitable accessories and the many details which proved to be involved in a project of this sort. Tourists would fill the hotels and cafés of the city. Coachloads of day trippers could be expected, and further parking facilities had to be provided below the city walls.

'Of course, we shall want someone to play Beatrice,' Cesare said, as the family were dining together one evening.

Amanda was dreamily savouring the creamy sauce in which her veal had been served. She was slow to realise that everyone was staring at her, and even slower to realise why.

Then a pink blush spread from her throat to her cheeks and up to her temples. 'No!'

'You're perfect,' Piero breathed. 'You look like her even in modern dress—we have always said so! In Renaissance costume you will be her double!'

Aunt Teresa agreed with him. 'Who else could do it? That hair, those eyes—it would not be easy to find a girl in San Volenco to match them! Our girls are usually so dark. Strange that Botticelli should always have painted such fair girls ...'

Lazily, Cesare said, 'You know his favourite model was the exquisite Simonetta, mistress of Giuliano de' Medici. She appears again and again in his canvases.'

'But our Beatrice was the wife of the Conte,' nodded Aunt Teresa. 'She was not a low-born woman of that sort!'

Piero laughed. 'Aunt, Simonetta was angelically beautiful, and it is no mean thing to be the mistress of one of the Medici! They expected wit as well as beauty; intelligence, too.'

Aunt Teresa shrugged, unimpressed. 'Still, it is strange that he should paint so many fair women.'

'He favoured their colouring,' agreed Cesare, staring coolly at Amanda. 'He was attracted by the combination of very blonde hair, almost silvery, and blue eyes. I think, myself, that he was influenced by the Hellenic revival. The Renaissance was brought into being by the admiration of our ancestors here in Italy for the classical models of the ancient Greek and Roman world. Botticelli's work reflects that cool Greek beauty; remote, almost abstract. When I was in Greece it was the quality of the cold, clear light that struck me—objects look much sharper and clearer there. That is the very feeling one gets from Botticelli.'

Piero shifted restlessly. He did not like the way in which his brother stared at Amanda. 'Myself, I think Botticelli is a great romantic. His paintings are so beautiful!'

Cesare grinned at Amanda. 'We have given you time to reconsider, haven't we? Now, how can you refuse to appear as the romantic and beautiful Beatrice, for Piero's sake?'

'I should feel a fool,' she disclaimed. 'Anyway, I thought there was some doubt as to who actually painted the picture?'

The family exploded with indignant denial. The Contessa said firmly, above their voices, 'Amanda, we have always said that it was by Botticelli. Art historians may say what they choose—to us it is a fact.'

Cesare laughed. 'So there!'

His mother reproved him with a look. 'Cesare, do not make fun of your mother.'

'No, Mamma!'

'But Aunt Maria, that costume,' Amanda protested. 'I could not wear it!'

The Contessa looked at Cesare, her brow troubled. 'The child is right. The costume is not suitable—it is too revealing.'

'All those gauzy draperies,' Amanda declared, grimacing.

'Surely no more revealing than a bikini,' Cesare shrugged. 'You have been known to wear one of those.'

'Privately,' she snapped.

'On the beach? Not so very private.' Cesare was wearing that look again, the sardonic amusement which maddened her.

'Among many other girls, however, whereas if I am appearing as Beatrice the crowds will all be staring at me and I shall feel very public indeed.'

'She is right, Cesare,' nodded Aunt Teresa anxiously. 'It is not seemly.'

'Especially for one of the family,' said the Contessa with a little frown.

'Why did Beatrice wear those clothes?' Aunt Teresa wondered aloud with a sigh. 'I thought they all wore the sort of clothes the Contessa Bianca is wearing in her portrait!' Contessa Bianca was another Renaissance figure. Her portrait, in a bold yellow brocade gown, dominated the centre of the picture gallery. She was a typical Druetso with silky black hair, olive skin and great dark eyes.

'Beatrice was dressed up as an allegorical figure,' the Contessa informed her tolerantly. 'She is supposed to be a nymph.'

'Oh,' said Aunt Teresa blankly.

'A nymph defying the wicked advances of a centaur,' Cesare expounded, tongue in cheek.

'I thought it was a horse,' said Aunt Teresa, open-mouthed.

They all laughed. Gently, Contessa Maria said, 'It is very dark in that corner. We must hang the portrait in a better light.'

After dinner they all trooped up to the gallery to view the Beatrice. The picture had a typical Renaissance background—a wood in spring; the dark leaves interlaced against a clear sky, with a city in the distance on a hilltop, a city clearly recognisable as San Volenco. The girl was poised for flight, her pale draperies fluttering in a breeze, her golden ringlets finely tossed around her delicate face.

Cesare leaned against the wall, looking from one to the other of them; from Amanda back to the portrait, then back to Amanda again.

'You are Beatrice,' he murmured.

Piero nodded eagerly. 'Yes, you are, *cara*. You cannot refuse to play the part—it would be a tragedy. You were born to do this!'

'At least the part doesn't include being thrown off the balcony to fall down to the valley floor,' Amanda said grudgingly. 'I suppose I ought to be grateful for that much.'

'We will make the draperies as modest as possible,' Cesare assured her.

'Thank you,' she said, a trifle tartly, thinking that he bore a strange resemblance to the dark-visaged centaur from whom the girl was in flight.

Two days later, Piero informed her that he was going to have to travel to Florence to take part in a conference of wine growers. Cesare was eager for the firm to take a place in the international market, hence Piero's original trip to England, to learn all he could about the London end of the business.

'This conference may mean orders,' Piero told her. 'I have to go.'

'I would love to see Florence again,' she said. 'While you are working I could sightsee. It will be marvellous to wander around the Uffizi, to see the Duomo again, and the Baptistery doors. Remember, it's five years since I saw them all.'

'I will ask Cesare,' Piero said doubtfully. 'I would love to take you, my darling, but you know how it is ... business conferences do not halt when it is five-thirty. They go on over dinner, even at breakfast each morning!'

Cesare was more forthright. 'You'll need all your wits about you on this trip, Piero. I can't have you distracted by the lovely Amanda. She can play the tourist in Florence some other time. There is plenty for her tò do here while you are away.'

Amanda was bitterly resentful when Piero reported this conversation to her.

'So, the Dictator of San Volenco says I shall not go,' she cried angrily. Cesare was a dark force at the back of everything that happened in the city; moving, manipulating, constantly in control of their lives.

'We must try to propitiate him, remember,' Piero pleaded. 'While I am away, darling, be nice to Cesare. Don't argue with him all the time.' He wore a harassed expression.

'Oh, Piero!' she sighed.

'You bring out the worst in him,' he explained. 'Cesare is not the dictator you think him. It is just that he has always been the head of the family, and he is used to making the decisions for all of us. When you cross him he is baffled. He only thinks for our good.'

'Piero——' she began shyly, trying to find words to convey her nervousness where Cesare was concerned. But what could she say? She was not even sure, herself, what it was about Cesare that made her so anxious. Piero loved his brother. He would not believe evil of him. He clearly resented it if Cesare paid attention to Amanda, but he seemed to feel few doubts as to the wisdom of leaving his fiancée in close relationship with a man who had once proposed to her, and still showed signs of resenting their own betrothal.

He trusts Cesare, Amanda thought, looking at his handsome, boyish face as he kissed her.

'Where will you stay in Florence?' she asked.

'In the Via dei Pilastri with some old friends of mine,' Piero told her.

'Oh, not in a hotel?'

'No, not in a hotel.'

'Good friends of yours? Do I know them?'

A slight flush rose in his cheeks. She was puzzled by it. 'No,' he faltered, 'I don't think you know them.'

Cesare came into the room unexpectedly. He looked at Piero with a raised brow, searching his brother's flushed face curiously. 'Who does Amanda not know?'

'The people Piero is going to stay with in Florence,' she told him.

Cesare looked sharply at Piero. 'Aren't you going to the Hotel Maggiore?'

'No,' said Amanda, as Piero was slow to reply. 'He is staying in the Via dei Pilastri with some friends.'

Piero was crimson. Cesare stared at him, his brows drawing together in a black line.

'I thought I made myself clear?' Cesare demanded. 'I

told you to go to the Maggiore. You have gone behind my back, after all, have you? How dare you do this? I made it quite clear to you how things were to be in future...'

Amanda was dumb with amazement at Cesare's angry, domineering tone. She looked at Piero incredulously, waiting for him to reply forcefully.

Piero was pale now. He stared at his feet. 'I know what you said. You said it often enough.'

'Then you will revert to the original arrangements,' Cesare commanded. 'You will go to the Hotel Maggiore.'

Piero shrugged. 'Just as you say...'

When Cesare had gone, Amanda demanded angrily, 'Why did you let him order you about like that? You are no longer a child, never permitted to think for yourself. Why shouldn't you stay with friends? I suppose Cesare doesn't approve of them? He thinks they will be a bad influence on you? Oh, Piero, if you never stand up to him you'll be a boy all your life...'

'Isn't it enough that I have my brother nagging me all day without you joining in as well?' Piero shouted. 'Leave me alone, Amanda. You don't know what you're talking about!'

She was horrified when he had gone. He was right— she had been nagging him. It was hard not to, though, when she saw how Cesare dominated him. For the first time she saw why Cesare had said that they would be ill-suited. Piero was a plastic personality, easy-going, sweet-tempered. He hated quarrels, detested trouble of any kind. Although he longed to prove to his family that he was an adult, he always sheered off from any contest which might actually prove his maturity.

She covered her face with her hands. How dare I criticise poor Piero? He is marrying a termagant. I am marrying an angel. I should be grateful for his sweetness, not condemn him for it.

She apologised when they next met, kissing him lovingly. 'Forgive me, darling?'

He returned her kiss eagerly. 'It was my fault. I was angry with Cesare and I shouted at you. You were right—I am weak. I will try to be stronger for your sake.'

'You aren't weak, Piero,' she denied. 'You are so much younger than Cesare that you've acquired a habit of obedience, that's all.'

He laughed bitterly. 'A habit of obedience! Yes, that is it, Amanda!'

'You should stand up to him. Go to your friends! Don't stay at the Maggiore. Don't let him choose your friends for you. It's your life, not his . . .' Her own views were coloured by a conviction that Cesare would attempt to put an end to their engagement with the same firmness which he had used in dictating Piero's friendships. If Piero abandoned old friends at Cesare's dictate, he might be as weak where she was concerned.

Piero gazed at her oddly, rather pale. 'You do not understand, my darling . . .'

'I understand Cesare,' she nodded. 'You're a man now. If you really like these people then refuse to give them up. Trust your own judgment. If you think Cesare's reason for disliking them is sound, of course, that's different. But it must be your decision.'

'Yes,' Piero said slowly, 'you are right. It is my decision, not Cesare's . . .'

When it was time for him to leave the family assembled to see him off, but Cesare refused to give Amanda permission to walk down to the car park to see him drive away. 'Piero must be on his way quickly. I want no protracted goodbyes.'

'You big bully,' she said scornfully.

Piero kissed her lightly, inhibited presumably by his brother's watchful presence, and was soon gone. Leaving the Contessa and Aunt Teresa in the hall, Amanda bolted upstairs and leaned on the windowsill of the office tower, watching for Piero's car. After a while she saw it moving across the plain. She watched until it was just a cloud of dust.

When she moved away from the window Cesare was seated at his own desk, reading a list of horse shows which had come in that morning's post. He looked at her, level-browed.

'Is parting such sweet sorrow still?' A cynical smile sounded in his voice.

'Oh, shut up!'

'You always sound defensive when you shout. Wish you were going with him? Or relieved not to be?'

'You put your own poisonous interpretations on most things,' she snapped. 'What do you think?'

'I think you were feeling lost and bewildered in England. You may be half English, but this is your real home. You fought down that homesickness because your stubborn mind would not admit to it.'

'Quite the little psychiatrist, aren't you?' she said with a sarcastic bite.

'So that when you saw Piero again you clutched at him, as a drowning man clutches at a lifeline.'

'What nonsense!' she said angrily.

He swung reflectively in his chair, his hands linked behind his tilted head, the mocking grey eyes watching her.

'Like most women, you have a tendency to leap emotionally at the first pretty thing that takes your fancy. In this case, Piero, my cherished brother. Only as an afterthought do you wonder if it is really something you need—the thing you should have chosen, the necessary thing.'

She turned away, fighting down a sudden desire to burst into tears which baffled her. After a pause she gasped, 'I love him!'

'Do you?' he drawled. 'I wonder.'

'What do you know of love?' she demanded bitingly.

He smiled lazily. 'I suspect I know a great deal more than you! Tell me, Amanda, how many men have kissed you?'

The question threw her. She stared at him dumbly for a moment, then, pulling herself together, she said, 'I don't know! Quite a few, I suppose!'

'Which means what? One or two? Half a dozen?'

'I didn't make notches on my belt,' she declared crossly.

'Was it ever serious?' He sounded quite dispassionate.

'Once or twice.'

'Did you touch the depths, or reach the heights?' The question came sharply, like a darting thrust of a rapier.

She shrugged, flushing. 'Don't we all at some time or another?'

'It can be shattering, can't it?' He watched her cynically. 'Like being poleaxed—you go down, stars whirling round your head, and you don't know what's happened to you at first.'

'Don't tell me you've ever felt like that, because I wouldn't believe you if you swore it on a stack of Bibles ten feet high. You're too cold-blooded to fall in love. You've never lost control, you've never lost your head. Piero and I are fools enough for that—we're human beings. But you are the Count of San Volenco and you're above such human weaknesses.' She spat the words out breathlessly, glaring at him, her face very pink.

He laughed. 'You really have a high opinion of me, don't you? I ought to feel insulted, but oddly enough I don't...'

'Of course not. Your own opinion of you is so high!'

'Sheathe those kitten claws now, my dear,' he said softly. 'Or I might retaliate!'

'Fling me off the balcony? Slap my face? Put me in the castle dungeons in chains?' She mocked him angrily. 'What will you do to me, my lord Dictator of San Volenco?'

He caught her by the wrists, his fingers iron links around her fragile bones, and pulled her towards him.

Too late Amanda tried to struggle away. His grip was unbreakable. His dark face came down towards her like a hawk swooping from the sky on a white dove. She was first angry, then frightened, then, finally, touched into response as his kiss burned along her lips, giving and demanding sheer physical pleasure.

Her hands were released, he slid his grip along her arms to her shoulders, then down her back to her waist, bending her backwards, his pressure irresistible. She flung up her hands and beat, unavailingly, upon the hard muscles of his chest.

'Don't fight me,' he whispered, his lips travelling slowly along her throat until they reached the small hollow, just above the curve of her breasts, where a pulse leapt wildly, testifying to the confusion of her senses.

'Let me go, Cesare,' she begged.

He laughed. 'Have you forgotten what the Counts of San Volenco have always been called? The hawks who never let go ... that is what they called us!' He looked down at her broodingly, his mouth curved in a cruel smile. 'How does it feel to be the prey of a hawk, *cara*?'

A half sob broke from her. 'Don't!'

'What did you say to me just now? That I never lost my head? That I was above human weaknesses?' He lowered his lips to her throat again, let them move slowly, with a burning intensity, downwards until they rested between her breasts, pushing aside the lapels of her shirt to reveal her smooth white skin. 'I warned you I would retaliate if you provoked me too far. Women are never satisfied until they have provoked a man to the point of madness, are they? Did you think I was a machine, bloodless, inhuman, that you came back here flaunting your betrothal to Piero, my own brother?' His voice was husky with emotion. Was it anger or pain? she wondered urgently. She tried to read the dark mask of his face, but it was still impossible for her to decipher what lay behind his hawklike features.

Tentatively, she said, 'But you only proposed to me to please your mother. It can't have hurt you when I refused!'

He raised his head reluctantly, as if he hated to look at her. 'What do you know of me, Amanda? You talk blithely about what I feel or cannot feel, but what do you really know of me? You're a child, emotionally, unable to recognise or understand any feelings deeper or more complicated than her own. You aren't old enough to marry anyone. You lack the maturity to comprehend another person in the total fullness of marriage.'

'That isn't true,' she cried angrily. 'I've been in love before, I know what it feels like ... and I do love Piero!'

'Do you?' he asked her savagely, his eyes on the trembling curve of her red mouth. 'I've seen you together, remember, and I have seen you kiss him.' His eyes flashed bitter mockery at her. 'The sweet childlike kisses of adolescents! They may satisfy Piero, but they would not satisfy me!'

'Of course not,' she flung back furiously, wounded by his sarcasm, her pride and self-respect stung. 'What would satisfy you, Cesare? Who could satisfy the Hawk of San Volenco?'

'Not you, at any rate,' he said bitingly. 'This exquisite, fragile body of yours conceals a frightened child, unable to give or receive adult love. I pity Piero.'

'Pity yourself if I tell him how you have behaved,' she said shakily. 'He'll kill you.'

He smiled darkly. 'And will you tell him?'

She bit her lip. 'Yes ... no! I don't know. I ought to tell him, warn him what sort of man his wonderful brother really is ... he has no idea, does he? He respects you, looks up to you, and all the time you are capable of this sort of treachery!'

He looked at her with anger, his grey eyes almost black with the mounting rage he felt. 'If I have betrayed Piero it is because I feel no cause to be loyal to him ... Piero knew when he brought you back as his fiancée that it would be a deadly insult to me, yet he went ahead and did just as he pleased. He knew I had chosen you as my Contessa ...'

'I refused you five years ago!' she cried.

His lip curled. 'What has that to do with it? Do you think I accepted your refusal as final? You were still a child, only just eighteen. We were all waiting for you to return, as you would have done, sooner or later. We did not expect you to return as Piero's future wife!'

'We ... you say we ... you only proposed to me for your mother's sake, as I said! It was always her dream that I would marry you, and you keep up the idea because you hate to be thwarted. It hurt your pride when I refused to fall in with your plans. I couldn't hurt your feelings because you don't have any ...'

'None that you are apparently able to comprehend,' Cesare agreed smoothly. He let his eyes move slowly over her. Amanda shivered at the sensual hunger his glance suddenly revealed, and his glance lifted sharply to her face, probing her eyes.

'So,' he murmured softly. 'Do you begin to understand me?'

Her face was suddenly burning, her eyes dropped nervously before his penetrating stare. Something in the way he looked at her had shown her what she had never suspected before ... Cesare might not be in love with her, but he desired her. His glance had told her that, reinforcing the revelation of his earlier kisses. She had thought at first that he had only been angry with her, that his lovemaking had been designed to insult and enrage her rather than to satisfy a hunger in him. Now she knew instinctively that Cesare wanted her, that she aroused the acquisitive instinct in that possessive spirit of his. The hawk, as he had said earlier, had scented his prey, and she shivered beneath the shadow of his wing.

'I ... I will marry Piero,' she stammered, avoiding his eyes. 'Leave me alone, Cesare, or I'll be forced to tell him that ... that...'

He laughed. 'That I want you, and intend to have you?'

She gasped at this outright statement of a fact she had only just recognised with embarrassed reluctance. 'Oh!' She broke away from him and ran from the room, hearing his soft laughter pursuing her as she fled.

CHAPTER FIVE

ALONE in her room, Amanda sat on the bed and stared at her pale reflection in the mirror. Her eyes looked enormous. Her mouth was trembling visibly and a little pulse beat at the base of her slender white throat.

Suddenly she remembered what Tina had said in the antique shop about Cesare's attitude to Piero's engagement. The words burned in her memory ... 'To his own mother the Conte said it—never while there is breath in my body ... this English girl will never marry Piero ...'

She shivered, covering her face with her hands. Tina's angry declaration now took on new and terrifying meaning. Cesare had not merely been speaking out of proud rejection of her marriage. He had still desired her for himself.

Beneath her cold fingers her skin glowed with sudden heat as her thoughts clarified. Wave after wave of scarlet colour swept up her face, then she lowered her hands and looked deliberately at herself. What was it about her that affected Cesare in this way? Why did he want her?

'I don't want him!' she cried aloud to the empty room, then bit her lip and looked round nervously, afraid of listeners outside. She felt like a small, hunted animal who suddenly becomes aware that the fox is on its trail. Every nerve-end in her body quivered with alarm.

Piero was away, and would be out of reach for a little

while. She dared not go to the Contessa for help—it would hurt her feelings too much. Aunt Teresa was too gentle, too kindly to be of much use, either.

There's no one, Amanda thought helplessly. I have no refuge to which I can run, no sanctuary to shelter in here. Cesare can always find me.

Then her chin lifted. I have myself, she thought proudly. I defeated him before, I can defeat him again. What can he do to me, after all, if I make it clear that I want nothing to do with him? He took me by surprise before. Now I'm warned, so I shall protect myself from him. There are ways of building walls around oneself, the invisible walls of cold rejection which every man recognises.

She stood up and began to brush her hair, then stiffened as she saw the shadowy bruises on her throat where he had angrily kissed and held her. 'Barbarian!' she said aloud. Her fingers touched the blue marks lightly. She had a flashing picture of herself in his strong brown hands, helpless as his mouth lingered at will on her lips, throat, shoulders. Her anger and contempt flared up. How dare he treat her in such a way? It was despicable.

He had even dared to imply that she had provoked him in some way, that his attack on her was justified by some action of her own! His reasoning was typically twisted. After all, she had refused to marry him. She had given him no encouragement since her return to the city. How then could he say that she had provoked him?

She washed her face in cool water, dried it slowly and carefully, then applied fresh make-up with fingers that trembled slightly. Then with a controlled expression she returned to Cesare's office, armed for battle.

It was an anti-climax to find it empty. She stood in the room without moving for a moment, then let out a long sigh.

For a second she was horrified by a suspicion that she was disappointed not to find him there—that she had been looking forward to a clash with him. Any faintest suspicion that she did not detest his very presence near her was enough to alarm her at the moment.

She asked herself silently why she was so determined to hate him, and knew, in her most secret soul, that it was a determination born out of that crushed-down attraction towards Cesare which she had felt as she saw his mouth coming down towards her own. Something hidden deep inside her had leapt into hot life, only to be beaten down once more by her mind.

She stood beside the window, staring down over the plain, and remembered. Remembered many times when she had shrunk back from the naked power of Cesare's presence, the domination of his personality. She would not be one of the moths drawn to that flame. She had seen too many other girls flutter away, singed. Even as a very young girl she had resisted the fatal attraction. The master of San Volenco was even more devastating to a very young girl, indeed. She had fled instinctively from him, as a dove flees the shadow of the hawk.

But I do love Piero, she told herself fiercely. I love him, and I will marry him—even if Cesare has said that I will be the dominant partner! I love Piero far too much to try to dominate him. Once he was away from Cesare's over-powering influence, surely Piero would grow stronger, become more assertive, both as a man and as a lover?

Cesare's bitter words about the kisses of adolescents had gone home, despite her angry denials to him at the time. It was true that Piero had never proved quite as passionate and demanding as she might have wished, but she was sure that in time that would change. Piero was all she wanted out of life...

Cesare did not appear again that day. Amanda worked in the office as usual on the details of the organisation of the Beatrice pageant, but found it hard to concentrate on such matters while her head was full of something very different. At every moment she expected Cesare to walk through the door. It was nerve-racking, and, she sus-pected, quite deliberate on his part. Cesare would be good at the game of cat-and-mouse.

She dressed carefully for the evening meal, her pulses leaping as she went down to join the rest of the family. Her glance skimmed the room, found his dark profile and hurriedly flickered away, the colour rising in her cheeks.

He was talking lazily to Aunt Teresa, teasing her. 'What part are you going to play in our pageant, then, Aunt? How about the Contessa Bianca?'

'You are joking, Cesare,' Aunt Teresa laughed, de-lighted.

'Who is going to play Bianca, my son?' asked his mother with a serious glance.

'Aunt Teresa,' Cesare insisted.

Contessa Maria smiled indulgently. 'But really ... who did you think most suitable?'

Cesare gave Amanda a quick, light look. 'I thought ... Tina...' There was mockery in the smile which accompanied the name.

'Oh, yes,' said Aunt Teresa. 'She will look exactly right!'

At that moment the girl herself came into the room; Amanda almost suspected Tina of eavesdropping. There was a strangely triumphant smile on the girl's beautiful, sulky face.

'Will you play the Contessa Bianca, Tina?' asked Cesare with a smile.

'Do you think I can play a Countess of Volenco?' asked Tina, her dark eyes wide and innocent. 'After all, I am not one of the family, am I? My ancestors were peasants, not noblemen!'

Cesare gave her an amused, appreciative smile. 'You're a lovely, warm-blooded little creature, Tina. What does it matter who your ancestors were? You look like Bianca. You'll play the part to perfection!'

Tina smoothed down the tight-fitting black skirt she wore, her fingers deliberately emphasising the curved swell of her hips. Cesare's glance followed the movement. His lips twitched with amusement.

'Well, if you want me,' Tina purred softly.

What exactly did she mean by that? wondered Amanda cynically. Something told her that Tina was not only referring to the part in the pageant.

Cesare looked at her directly. 'Have Tina measured right away. The costume for Bianca must be a perfect fit.'

'Will it be exactly the same as the painting?' asked Tina eagerly.

Cesare nodded. 'Exactly the same! The colour will suit you perfectly.' He slid an arm around her waist and added, 'Come and take a look at the portrait now.'

Amanda watched as he and Tina left the room. Contessa Maria was frowning in some puzzlement. She stared after her son, then looked at Amanda. For a second or two it looked as if the Contessa was going to make some remark about Cesare's sudden interest in Tina, then she clearly decided against saying anything, for she closed her lips firmly and looked uneasily at the sky beyond the window.

Amanda knew perfectly well why Cesare was being so attentive to Tina suddenly. His expression had told her the reason. He was demonstrating to her that other women found him irresistible ... as if she needed any further evidence! She had always known about his women. It had only intensified her own determination never to fall under his spell.

When Cesare and Tina returned, Tina had a faint flush along her cheekbones and a feline smile of satisfaction on her red mouth. She looked like a woman who has been kissed, and Amanda suspected that that was precisely what had happened up in the portrait gallery. Under the predatory eyes of the Druetso Counts their descendant had once more asserted his hereditary right to take what he wanted . . .

Some of the costumes were being hired from a costumier in Florence who specialised in this sort of thing, but others were being made to order here in San Volenco, where needlework of a fine sort was a favourite pastime of the local women. Their skills were hereditary, passed on from generation to generation, mother to daughter, and they had a fiercely competitive attitude to the finished article. The most accomplished needlewoman in the city was Signora Marella, a small, upright lady with greying dark hair and calm black eyes. Her hands moved softly, delicately, over the brocade she was using, like small brown moths hovering above the material. Amanda found it fascinating to watch.

'I myself will make your costume, Manda,' she was told firmly.

'Thank you, *signora*,' she said, delighted.

'It is to be exactly the same as the Beatrice portrait?' Signora Marella looked faintly disapproving.

Amanda nodded, smiling. She knew the other woman would not like the idea—the women of San Volenco were still old-fashioned in their attitudes to dress. Many of them still wore black every day in mourning for some relative or another. Old habits died hard in these quiet houses. The city walls which had once kept out invading armies now protected the people of the city from the modern invasion of new ideas.

Signora Marella clicked her tongue and shook her head. 'But the costume would show' . . . she lowered her voice discreetly . . . 'show the limbs . . '

'The Conte insists it be identical,' Amanda sighed.

Signora Marella gave her a brief glance. 'Ah, the Conte ... men! They never think ...'

'It will be very embarrassing,' Amanda confided. She was not looking forward to appearing in public wearing such flimsy clothes.

'We must see what we can do,' said the Signora. 'Let us look at the portrait again ...'

They went up to the gallery and stood in front of the picture. The Signora shook her head once more over the fluttering draperies.

'*Bellissima*, but ... too revealing ...'

Through the wisps of gauze the flesh of Beatrice glowed with a pearly smoothness which was sensual and riveting, but Amanda could not imagine herself looking like that. She shivered, staring at the dark wood behind the Beatrice, and the shadowy outline of the centaur, half horse, half satyr, pursuing her out of the darkness. All the light in the picture seemed to be concentrated around the girl's slight figure. This chiaroscuro gave the painting a somewhat ominous look, as if it symbolised the menace of darkness in pursuit of light.

'I wonder if the pursuer is Beatrice's husband?' she murmured to herself, not realising she spoke aloud.

From behind her Cesare said softly, 'Of course it is.'

She started violently, looking back at him with a haunted expression.

'Oh ... hello ...'

Signora Marella watched them curiously. Like the rest

of the city she knew exactly how the land lay between them.

'Cesare, Signora Marella agrees with me that the costume would not be decent . . .' Amanda said hurriedly.

'It will be exactly as Botticelli painted it,' Cesare said with a cold look.

Signora Marella shrugged. '*Si, Signore* . . .' She gave Amanda a look of wry resignation and slipped quietly away.

Amanda moved to follow her, cheeks flushed with alarm, but Cesare caught her by the arm and forced her to remain.

'Wait . . . I want a word with you!'

'I have a lot to do,' she protested.

He lifted one dark brow. 'Oh, indeed?'

She looked down, her poise shattered. He knew perfectly well that she had already got the work finished for that day. They had been working in the office together for several hours, and Cesare's quick, observant eyes must have noticed how little she had to do.

Cesare released her arm and moved back in front of the picture. 'Her flight did not take her far,' he murmured.

She looked up. His eyes were fixed on the picture. She stared at his dark profile; the unyielding hawk-like nose and chin, the hooded eyes, the strong, fierce mouth. Something beat hotly behind her eyes. She shivered, and he looked round at her.

Their eyes met in an armed clash, then Cesare's smile

deepened. 'You have such a look of·her,' he said softly. 'You always have had.'

'And you look like him,' she flung angrily, regretting it too late, for at the accusation he looked so amused.

'Is that so strange? He was my ancestor, another Hawk of Volenco...'

'He lost his prey that time, then,' she said triumphantly.

Cesare stared at her. 'What?'

'Beatrice escaped him, even if it was only by dying,' she pointed out.

'You forget, *cara*,' he said coolly, 'there are two versions of the legend. In one, it is true, she jumps to her death from the balcony of her room—your room, Amanda.' He smiled glitteringly at her. 'But in the other...' He moved closer, his hand lifting her chin and forcing her to look into his dark face. 'In the other the Hawk took his prey and kept her. They had children who were our ancestors, yours and mine ... how else could you have inherited her pale silvery hair and that other-world look which Botticelli loved as much as her Druetso lover did?' Cesare's eyes moved caressingly over her hair and face. His other hand gently slid over her head, stroking back the stray fronds of hair from her pale temples.

Huskily, she whispered, 'Cesare, please ... you mustn't,' but her voice was barely audible and she herself scarcely heard it above the thudding of her heart.

'Do you remember when you were a little girl and I took you to see the motto above the city gates?'

She nodded. 'Yes.' If only, she thought drowningly, he would stop moving his thumb along her cheekbones. She felt the passage of that thumb as if it left tracks of fire. Every touch made her shake, made her bones melt until she wondered how she managed to remain standing.

'You remember the motto?'

'Of course,' she said weakly.

'In life, fidelity . . . in death, fidelity,' he said deeply, his grey eyes fixed on her face. 'The Druetso family have always held by that motto, Amanda. What we have we hold, and we demand absolute fidelity in return.' His hands tightened on her shoulder, pulling her closer. 'I recognise no other claim on you—I give you fair warning. Piero knew perfectly well how we in the city felt about your future. When he brought you back here it was a gesture of defiance to me. He flung down the gauntlet; I shall pick it up.'

'What about me?' Amanda demanded, suddenly shaking off the dreamy trance in which his physical nearness had held her. 'Do I have no right to determine my own future?'

'You?' Cesare laughed, his white teeth cruel.

She went white with rage. 'How dare you laugh at me? You and Piero are not two dogs fighting over a bone. I'm a human being and I demand the right to choose my own husband . . .'

'There is no question of choice,' Cesare said calmly.

She glared at him. 'Oh, isn't there? That's what you think, my lord Count.'

'It is what I know,' he said. 'Do you think I would

have chosen to fall in love with a frightened child who
has no more idea of love than a rabbit?' His face grew
fierce and dark as he stared down at her. 'You knew
years ago that you wanted me, Amanda. You knew
before I proposed to you ... you pretended to yourself
that you hated me, but if you are honest with yourself
your feelings were far more complicated and far more
interesting! I'm too experienced not to recognise the
reality of a woman's reactions when I hold her, but you,
Amanda, you are a nervous child terrified by the impact
of passion inside yourself, and you have denied how you
felt about me even to yourself because your own feelings
terrify you ...'

She tried to laugh angrily. 'Are these the sort of fan-
tasies you use to bolster your vanity, Cesare? You can't
bear to accept that any woman might reject you, so
you've told yourself I'm just too frightened to admit I
really...' Her voice broke off huskily on a gasp. 'It's
sheer nonsense,' she went on quickly. She just could not
bring herself to say the words which had been on the tip
of her tongue.

'Is it?' He looked down at her tauntingly. 'Let's see,
shall we?'

'No!' she cried, pulling back from him. Panic en-
gulfed her, throwing her brain into total confusion.

Cesare's hands were too strong for her. He pulled her
closer, like a helpless doll, against his body. His
mouth moved downwards. Her wide eyes stared, hypno-
tised, at the strong curve of his lips as they approached,
then a wave of sudden heat swept over her. She fought

desperately to withstand it, but as his lips touched hers she felt her whole body weaken, grow warmly limp, curve towards his. Her hands fluttered out, touched his chest and crept upwards to his throat. Cesare made a sound of triumph deep inside his chest and his hands moved to her waist, pulling her hard against him.

Amanda sobbed defeat, her hands clinging at the back of his dark head, her body pliantly yielding to him as his hard lips wrung absolute response from her. She ceased to think, drowning in pleasure, her mind submerged beneath the tidal wave of passion which swept them both away.

When he drew back she clung to him still, eyes closed, her face lifted towards him.

'You are beginning to learn, aren't you, my darling?' He had a note of triumph still in his thickened voice. 'Now deny that you want me...'

She gave a heart-wrenching sigh and opened her eyes. After a moment she said faintly, 'I'm a woman. Of course I'm not unaware of you...'

His mouth lifted in mocking amusement. 'Do you want me to prove my point again, *cara*? How many times a day would you like me to show you how you feel about me?'

She flushed. 'All right,' she said bitterly. 'I ... I find you attractive—I admit it.'

'Generous of you,' he said drily.

'I've found plenty of other men attractive,' she said in a belligerent voice.

Cesare's dark eyes narrowed. 'Let me warn you, my

girl, not to boast of such things to me! I can be a jealous lover...'

'You ... aren't my lover,' she denied huskily.

'No?' He smiled, possessively, at her.

'No,' she insisted. 'And you never will be, Cesare. I still intend to marry Piero.'

'Feeling as you do about me?' His glance was scathingly contemptuous as he spat out the words.

'Yes!'

'You could not be so stupid,' he said. 'Do you really think my brother wants a wife who is in love with me? He would have to be a masochist to enjoy such a situation, and Piero is not a masochist, believe me.'

'I'm not in love with you,' she said patiently.

'You have already admitted it,' he reminded her.

'No! I admitted that I find you ... physically ... attractive,' she stammered.

'Ah, yes,' he said. 'Physically attractive ... how many sorts of love do you think there are, *cara*? It is love you feel for me, believe me.'

'I know one thing about love,' she said. 'It cannot be confused with hate. Or with contempt. Or with dislike. And I feel all three of those for you.' She drew away and stood upright, facing him bravely. 'I'm not trying to insult you, Cesare. I'm forced to be honest because you will not accept anything else. Very well: I've always disliked you. You're arrogant, interfering, domineering; you were brought up by your father to act like that. It isn't your fault, I suppose. The Hawk of San Volenco is not supposed to be a perfect, gentle knight. You have a family tradition of fierce tyranny behind you, and you grew up believing it it to be the pattern you must follow. Look at him...' gesturing at the Botticelli painting. 'That's what you understand ... the centaur pursuing a frightened virgin ... Well, that isn't what I want. I want an ordinary happy marriage with a husband who will be my friend and partner, not my master.'

He listened unsmilingly, watching her. After a moment he said, 'You still do not know yourself.'

'No, it's you who doesn't know me!'

He shook his head. 'There is no mystery, no magic, in the marriage you just described. It is prosaic, dull...'

'It's happy and safe,' Amanda said crossly.

'Ah, safe! Now there you are admitting something of the truth. You want a safe husband because you are frightened of anything more demanding. You haven't the courage to commit yourself to the stormy sea of love, so you opt to stay in the quiet security of harbour with some undemanding mouse of a husband.'

She laughed suddenly. 'I wouldn't describe Piero as a mouse, would you? He can be very passionate.'

Cesare's face went black with rage. He caught her shoulders and shook her violently. 'Passionate, is he? My God, Amanda, you ask for trouble. How dare you say that to me? You will drive me to do something I will be sorry for later...'

She felt a flutter of excitement in her stomach. Cesare's jealousy gave her a sense of power she had never felt before. She looked at him through her lowered lashes. He was certainly a handsome man, she thought reluctantly. There was a dark grandeur about him which was impressive, and the way he was looking at her now made her pulses race furiously.

'You forget,' she said sweetly, 'I'm engaged to Piero, you know, not to you ...'

They suddenly heard the click of heels approaching. Cesare straightened away from Amanda, smoothing out the angry look from his face.

They turned and saw the Contessa coming towards them, her face filled with apprehension. She looked at Cesare closely.

'My son, Piero just rang from Florence.'

Cesare looked blank. 'Yes?'

'He is bringing guests back with him,' the Contessa said nervously.

'What?' Cesare's brows jerked together.

'To see the Beatrice pageant,' the Contessa said.

'Who are these guests?' demanded Cesare.

His mother looked at him anxiously. 'The Americans,' she said gently.

'Hah!' Cesare spat out an exclamation of pure rage.

Amanda was puzzled. 'What Americans are these, Aunt Maria?' she asked tentatively.

The Contessa glanced at her, then at Cesare. 'They are some friends of Piero's,' she said.

'Not the friends in the Via dei Pilastri with whom he is staying at the moment?' asked Amanda curiously.

The Contessa nodded. 'Indeed, those are the friends he is bringing back with him!'

'He dares to bring them here?' demanded Cesare. 'Is he mad to do such a thing?'

'But why shouldn't he?' Amanda asked in bewilderment.

'This is Piero's home,' the Contessa pointed out to Cesare in a gentle voice.

'I will not have that man and his daughter in my house,' Cesare merely said fiercely. 'Again Piero defies me. The time is soon coming when he must learn once and for all who is master here.' He turned on his heel and strode away angrily.

Amanda looked at the Contessa. 'I don't understand. What is so wrong with these Americans?'

The Contessa laughed. 'It is quite simple, my dear. Cesare hates this man because Mr MacDonald bought the Mireze stables...'

Amanda's eyes widened. 'The Mireze stables? I remember Cesare always wanted to buy them! They had a famous breed of mares over there, didn't they, which Cesare wanted to cross with the Volenco strain?'

The Contessa nodded. 'It has been his ambition to do so for many years now. The Mireze horses are closer to the Arab strain than ours here ... ours have more bodily strength, but the Mireze horses are faster, more graceful. Cesare has always dreamed of buying out the Mireze family. When Giorgio Mireze died, Cesare began negotiations with his daughter, Caterina. I don't know what went wrong, but suddenly she sold out to this American, Hector MacDonald. Cesare was bitterly angry, and he has refused to have any dealings with Mr MacDonald ever since.'

'How typical,' said Amanda. 'Stubborn as a mule!'

The Contessa laughed. 'Cesare can be very obstinate, it is true.'

'And so Piero knows them well enough to stay in their house?' Amanda asked. 'I mean, they're obviously not strangers to the family?'

'No,' the Contessa admitted. 'We all know them. Mr MacDonald came here a year ago from England—he wanted to settle down over here in Europe.'

'He must be wealthy,' said Amanda.

'Very, of course! And generous. He pays good wages, so we have heard.' The Contessa smiled wryly. 'He has even lured away one of our stablemen to work for him at Mireze.'

'That wasn't very nice of him.'

'It was fair enough. The man came from Mireze in the first place. His family lived over there and he wanted to go back.'

'Cesare didn't like it, though,' guessed Amanda.

'Not at all! He was furious. I think he was particularly angry because he had been friendly with the MacDonalds in the first place, and he felt that they had betrayed him by buying Mireze.'

Amanda shivered. 'Yes, he would feel that. He has such a powerful sense of loyalties.'

The Contessa's gaze was shrewd. 'It is a family tendency. The whole city probably feels the same.'

Amanda met her eyes. 'I feel their disapproval every

These three exciting Harlequin romance novels are yours FREE!

Lucy Gillen sets this romance among the wild lochs and mountains of Scotland. **"A Wife for Andrew"** is a touching account of a young governess, her dour yet compassionate employer and the children in his care who suffer at the hands of a jealous woman.

In Betty Neels' **"Fate Is Remarkable"** Sarah's "marriage of convenience" is dramatically altered. Just as Sarah was getting ready to tell Hugo that she'd fallen in love with him, a lovely woman from Hugo's past shows up…

In **"Bitter Masquerade"** by Margery Hilton, mistaken identity is the basis of Virginia Dalmont's marriage. When Brent mistook her for her twin sister Anna, she wondered if her love was strong enough to make up for the deceit…

In the pages of your FREE GIFT Romance Treasury Novels you'll get to know warm, true-to-life people, and you'll discover the special kind of miracle that love can be. The stories will sweep you to distant lands where intrigue, adventure and the destiny of many lives will thrill you. All three full-length novels are exquisitely bound together in a single hardcover volume that's your FREE GIFT, to introduce you to Harlequin Romance Treasury!

The most beautiful books you've ever seen!

Cover and spine of all volumes feature distinctive gilt designs. And an elegant bound-in ribbon bookmark adds a lovely feminine touch. No detail has been overlooked to make Romance Treasury books as beautiful and lasting as the stories they contain. What a delightful way to enjoy the very best and most popular Harlequin Romances again and again!

A whole world of romantic adventures!

If you are delighted with your FREE GIFT volume, you may, if you wish, receive a new Harlequin Romance Treasury volume as published every five weeks or so—delivered right to your door! The beautiful FREE GIFT VOLUME is yours to keep with no obligation to buy anything.

Fill out the coupon today to get your FREE GIFT VOLUME.

Three exciting, full-length Romance novels, in one beautiful book!

FREE GIFT!

Dear Ellen Windsor:

Yes, please send my FREE GIFT VOLUME with no obligation to buy anything. If you do not hear from me after receiving my free gift volume, please mail me the second volume of Romance Treasury. If I decide to keep the second volume, I will pay only $4.97 plus 39¢ for shipping and handling (total cost $5.36). I will then be entitled to examine other volumes at the rate of one volume (3 novels) every five weeks or so, as they are published. Each volume is at the low price of $4.97 plus 39¢ for shipping and handling (total cost $5.36) and comes to me on a 10-day free-approval basis. There is no minimum number of books I must buy. I can stop receiving books at any time simply by notifying you. The FREE GIFT VOLUME is mine to keep forever, no matter what I decide later.

Please print clearly.

C78 – 6R

_____

Name

_____

Address

_____

City   Province   Postal Code

Romance Treasury

Offer expires December 31, 1978.

time I walk through the streets.'

The Contessa nodded. 'They have a black-and-white attitude to such things!'

'And you? How do you feel?' asked Amanda.

The Contessa kissed her gently. 'I love you, my darling child. I am sure it will all work out for the best.'

Amanda did not ask her what she meant exactly. She preferred not to know.

Instead, she said, 'Now I understand why Cesare forbade Piero to stay in their house. But I do think he's being very tyrannical, all the same. I'm glad I advised Piero to do what he wanted to do and to take no notice of Cesare's opinions.'

The Contessa eyed her thoughtfully. 'Oh, you advised Piero to stay with them after all, did you?'

'Surely you, at least, agree that Cesare had no right to order Piero about like that?'

'Perhaps you do not see all the picture,' the Contessa said gently. 'Sometimes, my darling, Cesare has reasons which are very good ones, but which he does not communicate to you. There is more to this business than a simple dislike of the MacDonalds.'

'What else is there, then?' asked Amanda bluntly.

The Contessa sighed. 'You must ask Piero,' she said.

CHAPTER SIX

EVERY morning at sunrise Amanda and Cesare took their morning ride together across the sun-baked plains of the valley below the city. Amanda took care to get up on time each morning, knowing that if she ever forgot, Cesare would not hesitate to stride into her room in search of her. Remembering that first morning, when he had so suddenly arrived to wake her, she wished to avoid any repeat performance, with herself only scantily clad in her brief nightdress, blushing like a teenager under Cesare's dark gaze.

She was determined to avoid occasions that held suggestions of intimacy. She had thought long and deeply about her feelings, and come to the conclusion that the physical attraction he exerted did not make any difference to her views of him as a man. Cesare had medieval attitudes towards women. He did not see them as equals. They were either playthings or chattels to him. He would make any modern, independent woman an intolerable husband.

'I want to be free,' she told herself fiercely. 'I want to be my husband's equal, his partner, not his slave...'

When they returned from their ride they had breakfast, then worked in the office each day on the plans for the Beatrice pageant.

They were beginning rehearsals for the pageant now.

The costumes were ready at last, and Cesare called a dress rehearsal one morning, the day before Piero was due to return home with his American guests.

Tina was excited as she began to insert herself gingerly into the many petticoats which she would have to wear beneath the bold yellow costume which was the replica of Contessa Bianca's dress. Her black eyes snapped triumphantly as she looked at herself in the long mirror which had been brought down into the breakfast room. They were going to parade in front of Cesare, his mother, Aunt Teresa and the servants who were all gathered together in the great hall to watch the fascinating procession.

Swirling around the room, her skirts flying, Tina crowed softly to herself.

'Now I look like a Contessa!'

Amanda was feeling very unhappy. She shivered in her drifting wisps of gauze, feeling naked and exposed. She hugged herself with her arms around her chest, crossed defensively over her half-bared breasts, and decided she could not go out into the hall to be stared at by . . . by anyone.

Tina came to a halt and looked at her, brows drawn. Her black eyes were narrowed in sudden temper. 'You look ridiculous,' she snapped.

Signora Marella clicked her tongue. 'Silence, girl! How dare you say such things?' She gently unwound Amanda's hands and made her stand less awkwardly. '*Bellissima*,' she murmured.

'Tina's right. I look silly!'

'You look very beautiful,' said the Signora firmly. 'Come!'

'I can't go out there...'

Tina laughed. 'She is a coward! She feels as silly as she looks, you see!'

The Signora urged them all into a line. There were half a dozen other women, all dressed in the rich costumes of past Druetso women, and they chattered excitedly as they began to move out into the hall. Amanda hung back nervously, her teeth chattering.

'Come,' ordered the Signora. 'Lift your head ... do not walk like a sack ... relax ... remember, you are beautiful...'

Amanda began to walk, her head lifted as the Signora ordered. She was the last in the procession. As she glided along her gauzy draperies fluttered back to reveal the long line of her white thighs, her waist supple and slender, the pearly gleam of her breasts lifting clear of the thin material. She was wearing a coronet of spring flowers; palest pink buds, green leaves, golden flowers. On her fine silvery fair hair the coronet conferred a touch of magic. Even her nervousness improved her, giving her cheeks a delicate pallor which was enchanting.

Cesare stood in the hall, partly in shadow, his black head thrown back arrogantly as he surveyed the women parading in front of him. He looks like a slave-master inspecting the latest batch of slave girls, thought Amanda savagely. I detest him! He's a beast...

Then the grey eyes moved on to her, widened abruptly. She saw his nostrils flare, his lips part on a hungry sigh.

Her own body shook with a sudden answering passion. They looked at each other in a silence which had the quality of music—emotion flowed between them in a silver stream. At last Amanda tore her eyes away from him in self-hating bitterness. Her whole nature seemed to be eternally tortured, split between love and hatred, between desire and contempt. She was weary of the struggle. She suddenly longed to get away from the city, to escape back into the safe tedium of London's anonymous streets.

Everyone was waiting for Cesare to pronounce his verdict. After a long pause he said huskily, 'It is excellent. You agree, Mamma?'

'Yes,' the Contessa said doubtfully. 'Oh, indeed, excellent, but ...' Her gaze went to Amanda.

Signora Marella nodded. 'But the Beatrice costume is very revealing ...' she said with a triumphant smile. 'I thought it would be so ...'

Cesare's eyes went to Amanda again with a narrowed gaze. 'Yes,' he said. 'I will compare it with the painting before I make a decision.' He smiled at the other women. 'You are all perfect, though. Thank you. You can take your costumes off now.'

Tina swished towards him, her eyes inviting. Standing close to him, her breasts full and rounded beneath the yellow brocade of the bodice, she asked, 'And my costume? Do I make a good Contessa Bianca?'

Cesare smiled in appreciative amusement. 'You're ravishing, Tina,' he said softly.

She gave him a fluttering look. 'Really? You are not just flattering me?'

He laughed. 'You're a minx,' he retorted. 'Go on, change back into those everlasting jeans of yours. You look good whatever you wear, you know that all too well!'

Tina laughed back at him, flounced to the door and vanished. Signora Marella followed her. Amanda moved after them, but Cesare said coolly, 'No. We must compare you with the painting and decide whether the costume will do or not.'

Reluctantly, she followed him up to the gallery. They stood before the picture. His grey eyes moved from her to the picture, then back again. She felt the touch of his glance as if he held her between those strong brown hands once more.

'No,' he said, at last. 'Signora Marella has made the costume an exact replica, but I cannot bear the thought of other men seeing you in it ... It must be altered.'

Amanda turned away, relieved by his decision. She had been dreading the very idea of appearing in public like this ... Cesare caught her back, catching her wrist in his iron grasp.

'Don't go,' he said huskily. 'Let me look at you again.'

She could not bear his gaze. 'Don't,' she begged. 'You make me feel ... naked ...'

His smile was triumphantly possessive. 'Do I?' He ran his glance down the curve of her body. 'Do you know what you look like when you walk in that? You are as near to nakedness as it is possible to be wearing clothes, yet each movement both conceals and reveals, so that one is tantalised and enchanted at one and the same time.'

'I must go,' she said in despair. His nearness was making that shameful weakness creep over her again. She was determined not to give in to the need for him, the desire to be held in his arms, to feel his mouth on hers.

Cesare looked down at her searchingly. 'Very well,' he said. 'Run away, little rabbit. Tell Signora Marella to make the dress far less revealing.' He grimaced. 'I had not realised how much I would resent the thought of others seeing you half-naked. I was too eager to see you myself.'

She flushed. 'Cesare! Please ... leave me alone ... Stop persecuting me!'

He laughed mockingly. 'Stop what? My dear girl, you want me as much as I want you, and one day you will come to me and admit as much. One day you'll give in and stop running away.'

'I won't,' she denied. 'I shall never submit—never! You might as well stop trying to force me to do so, Cesare. My mind is not as weak as my body, remember. My intelligence tells me that we are not meant for each other.' She looked at him seriously, willing him to listen to her. 'You said so yourself, remember? You said I was too spirited, too forceful?'

'I said you were too spirited for Piero,' he corrected. 'Piero could not ride my horse, either—it would run away with him, or throw him! It is the same with women as with horses. They need the right master.'

'You will never be my master!' she flung furiously at him.

Cesare smiled. 'We shall see...'

Next morning they rode together as usual. Tina flirted with Cesare as she adjusted his stirrups, her thick dark lashes lowered one moment, raised the next, her black eyes teasing and inviting him.

'How do you expect me to work with my head filled with thoughts of the Pageant?' she demanded. 'I am too excited to pretend that all is normal. One moment I am just your stable girl, the next I am a Contessa...'

'You look exquisite in both parts,' Cesare told her calmly. 'Even in jeans, I admit, although I do not like to see women in such clothes.'

Tina glanced at Amanda. 'Or in jodhpurs?'

Cesare gave Amanda a sidelong little smile. 'On some women jodhpurs can be exciting.'

Tina bit her lip jealously, tossed her black hair and turned away with a pout.

'Now you've annoyed her,' Amanda said as they rode down through the sleeping city.

Cesare grinned. 'She is too blatant.'

'Isn't that what men like? That flashy sexuality?'

'You have feline instincts, do you?' Cesare looked amused. 'No, men do not necessarily like what you call flashy sexuality.' His dark glance drifted over her slight, boyish figure in a crisp white shirt and jodhpurs. 'Sometimes the very opposite can be more exciting. An ice maiden can always be melted.'

Amanda flicked her crop at Vesta's hindquarters, and the mare shot forward at a gallop.

They rode at full canter over the fields where some of the other Volenco horses grazed. Some of the mares lifted their heads as they heard the sound of hooves, and stared after them, nostrils flared with excitement.

Cesare rode level with Amanda, then drew away, leaving her behind easily. Viva's ears quivered, as if he read his master's mind, then he gave a deep-chested whinny, which Vesta answered softly, tossing her pretty head.

Amanda smoothed her horse's neck, her hand lingering on the silky mane. 'Silly creature,' she murmured. 'Ignore him!'

Later, Cesare said to her, 'Are you looking forward to Piero's return?'

'Of course,' she said defiantly.

'No doubt he'll want to know if you have missed him.' Cesare's voice was bland.

'And I shall tell him I have,' she said.

'Liar,' Cesare mocked.

She glared at him. 'It's true!'

'You barely noticed he wasn't here,' Cesare drawled.

She ignored him, her expression cold. They returned to the stables side by side, in total silence. Tina gave them a curious, penetrating look as she took the reins. Amanda stalked past her without saying anything, but Cesare paused to make some smiling comment before following Amanda's slight figure up to the castle. She was vanishing into the upper regions of the building as he paused in the great hall to speak to his mother.

'Cesare, I am worried,' began the Contessa gently.

'About what, Mamma?'

'About the situation...'

'Which situation?'

'Ah, you know very well what I mean!'

He smiled blandly. 'Do I?'

'You and Amanda,' the Contessa hinted.

'Ah, Amanda!' His eyes flashed hungrily. 'That situation ... it is all under control, Mamma.'

She gave him a long, anxious look. 'Under control, Cesare? I do not think so. I think you lose control more and more often these days. I have never seen you like this. Sometimes I have noticed a look almost of terror on the child's face, and I love Amanda dearly, my son. I do not like to see her so disturbed. She is so very young and gentle...'

'Do not worry about Amanda, Mamma,' he said haughtily. 'Amanda is my concern.'

'Cesare, don't shut me out! What is happening between you? She is still betrothed to your brother. What will Piero think? What will he say when he realises?'

'Piero must understand that he had no right to come between Amanda and myself. You know very well why he did it!' Cesare spoke between clenched teeth, his face taut with anger. 'He was punishing me. He wanted to hurt me. He knew what he did.'

The Contessa sighed. 'Piero is weak and he believes he has a grievance against you, Cesare. He resents your authority. He wished to prove something to you when he brought Amanda back here as his fiancée!'

'He wanted to drive me insane,' said Cesare in a sudden dark rage, his eyes glittering, his mouth taut. 'And he might yet succeed, with Amanda's help.'

He turned on his heel and strode up the stairs, and his mother watched him go helplessly, her face distracted. She wrung her hands and made a soft, keening sound, staring at nothing for a long while, her eyes bright with unshed tears.

Piero arrived home later in the afternoon, just as Amanda was leaving the office with Cesare. Cesare paused at the door, listening, then went to the window, and Amanda followed him. Together they stared down at the car as it came closer, dustily travelling over the plains.

'Piero,' Amanda sighed.

Cesare's thick dark brows drew together. 'Your beloved,' he drawled in bitter mockery.

Their eyes clashed. Hers fell first, before the fierce demand in his grey ones, and her colour mounted. She turned away, and he made no attempt to stop her as she left the room to meet Piero in the great hall. The Contessa was already there, with Aunt Teresa, anxious expressions on both their faces as they greeted her.

'You will meet Piero here? You will not go down to the gates to welcome him?' the Contessa asked her.

'I'll wait with you,' said Amanda. She was not eager to see Piero again. She felt guilty and uneasy, almost as if he would read in her face what had happened during his absence.

When Piero did arrive he was not alone. An older man walked on one side of him, dwarfing him, the red crest of his head flaunted cheerfully above a tweed jacket of unmistakable Scottish design. On the other side of Piero walked a girl, almost the same height as him, but with hair slightly paler in shade than her father's, and a skin of translucent purity and whiteness.

Amanda glanced at them politely while the Contessa moved forward to greet them.

'Hector! And Magdalen ... my dears, how delightful to see you again...' Her cheerfulness was slightly forced, but her welcoming smile was genuine, although anxiety underlay it.

'I'm certainly glad to see you again, Maria,' said Hector MacDonald in his broad American accent. 'It's been too long. I was beginning to be afraid I would never visit at Volenco again.' He grinned as he spoke, but his eyes were sober, and they glanced around the hall as he spoke, searching for someone who was absent. 'Where's Cesare?'

'He will be here in a moment,' the Contessa said. She kissed the other girl. 'Magdalen! How charming you look. Cream suits you so well...'

It was true, thought Amanda. The American girl was wearing a cream linen suit cut on superbly simple lines. The colour toned down the flame of her hair and reflected the smoothness of her skin. As she kissed the Contessa on both cheeks she was looking at Amanda over the older woman's thin shoulders, and Amanda was aware of a shadowy sadness in the other girl's pale green eyes.

The Contessa turned to draw Amanda forward. 'And this is our dearest Amanda...'

Magdalen MacDonald smiled slightly and held out a thin hand. 'How do you do? You're English, aren't you?'

'Half English,' corrected the Contessa quickly. 'She is a Druetso, too.'

'Of course,' said Magdalen on a dry note. 'How could I have forgotten? She's a Druetso.'

Amanda's quick ears picked up the note of wry sarcasm, and she wondered at it. For some reason Magdalen did not like her too well, she suspected. They had never met before. What reason could this girl have for not liking her?

She shook hands with Hector MacDonald, receiving an incredulous stare. 'Say, you remind me of ... hey! She's the image of that picture of yours, isn't she?'

'The Botticelli? But of course,' said the Contessa.

'She is playing the Beatrice in the Pageant,' said Piero, speaking for the first time. 'I told you, don't you remember?' He came forward to kiss Amanda briefly on the cheek. His eyes met hers only for a second or two. Was it her own guilty imagination, or did Piero look angry?

'You told us she was playing Beatrice, but you didn't tell us to expect such a perfect resemblance,' said Hector jovially. 'It's quite unbelievable!'

'She is a Druetso, after all,' said Magdalen sardonic-
ally.

Piero gave her a quick look. He was very pale. 'Even
as a little girl Amanda was the image of the portrait,' he
said. 'I remember Cesare used to make her stand beside it
so that he could look at them both together.'

Magdalen stared at Piero. 'Really!' Her voice was still
coldly sarcastic.

'Cesare was obsessed with her,' said Piero.

The Contessa looked at him in pale astonishment.
'Magdalen, my dear,' she broke in hurriedly, 'you will
want to see your room. Teresa will take you and your
father upstairs. You must need to wash after that long
journey.' Conversationally, leading them towards the
stairs with gentle inexorability, she added, 'How was
Florence? As charming and civilised as ever? You must
tell us how the city is looking these days later. I never get
there any more—I am too old.'

'Oh, no, Contessa,' Magdalen said softly. 'You are not
too old. You are still awe-inspiring...'

'Thank you, my dear,' said the Contessa with a little
sigh. 'I do my best.'

When they had reached the top of the stairs Magdalen
looked back at them. Amanda saw how her eyes touched
briefly on Piero's face, then moved away, and a sudden
suspicion flashed into her mind.

Piero said uneasily, 'Well, I had better go up and
freshen myself in my room, too, Amanda *mia*...'

'We must talk,' she said.

'Not now,' Piero murmured.

'As soon as possible,' she said, her suspicions growing as she realised that he was not meeting her eyes.

She left the hall, needing time alone in which to think, and slowly wandered down the narrow streets of the city, pausing here and there to stare at the tiny windows, crammed with souvenirs and postcards, with offers of tea or egg and chips for the tourists. From time to time she exchanged a smile or a greeting with one of the citizens. The air was warm and scented this evening, filled with the fragrance of summer. Above the city soared a sky still deeply blue, cloudless and bright.

Outside Giulio's antique shop she bumped into Tina. The other girl gave her one of her sullen looks, then said spitefully, 'So Piero has brought his American girl back with him? You are not the only Druetso who can have two strings to their bow, are you?'

Amanda looked back at her quietly. 'You see a lot of Giulio, don't you?'

Tina flushed. 'So what?'

Amanda shrugged. 'Nothing.'

Tina glared at her and walked away. Amanda carried on down the hill, her mind racing as she considered the implications behind Tina's words. Discarding the obvious spite involved, there was still sufficient evidence to back up what Tina had said. It would not surprise Amanda if Piero had had some sort of relationship with Magdalen MacDonald. It would explain her sarcasm towards his engagement. It would explain why Piero had been embarrassed. Pehaps, after all, he had not suspected

Amanda and Cesare. He had been feeling guilty himself because of Magdalen.

There had been that look between them as Magdalen stood at the top of the stairs. Even at a distance Amanda had seen the unhappiness and challenge in the other girl's eyes.

Sighing, she turned and sauntered back up the city. She made her way to the private garden and sat down on one of the seats, her eyes closed, breathing in the flowery scents, listening to the evening chorus of the birds in the ivy.

Something light and fragrant trailed across her cheek, touching her mouth at the corner. She smiled, her eyes tight shut.

'Is it you? I thought you would come to me here—it is our secret place, isn't it? Aren't you going to kiss me, darling?'

As his shadow blotted out the evening sunshine from her face she knew, with that instinct which betrays the presence of the hawk to the quivering prey, but it was too late. His mouth took hers by storm, angry, bitter, insulting.

She struggled to escape him, her lips stinging and bruised by the fierce pressure, but he would not let her go until he had awoken the sleeping hunger in herself which she so despised and crushed down. Then, as she involuntarily began to kiss him back, the tears of shame and self-detestation springing to her eyes. Cesare at last released her.

He looked down at her contemptuously. 'You should

be careful when you issue such invitations. What man could resist?'

'I hate you ... damn you!' she sobbed.

'If what you feel for me is hatred, then that is what I want,' he said silkily.

She silently glared at him. There was dark colour in his cheeks and he was not smiling. She sensed a change in him, and wondered what it meant.

'Sometimes, my little rabbit, I could pounce upon you and shake you until you beg for mercy,' he said crisply. 'Your ostrich attitude is beginning to annoy me. It is time you woke up.'

'First I'm a rabbit, then an ostrich,' she said. 'Make up your mind.'

'I think there is a little of the tigress buried in you somewhere, too,' he said softly. 'I would like to see it from time to time...'

Amanda turned away and went back towards the house. 'You know I thought you were Piero,' she said. 'It was not right to take advantage of my mistake.'

He walked beside her. 'Did Piero ever kiss you until you were half mad with pleasure?'

'I would not want him to,' she said angrily.

Cesare laughed. 'Little liar. You want it, all right.'

She tensed, her hands balling into fists. 'Don't call me a liar again!'

'Are you going to hit me?' Cesare was amused. He paused and looked down at her. Pointing at his chin, he said, 'Here...'

She was so angry that her control slipped. Her hand

flew up and struck him, hard, across the cheek.

He blinked, surprised and taken off balance, then laughed harshly. A red mark glowed on his cheek where she had struck him.

'One day we'll have a showdown, you and I,' he said softly.

Amanda fled from him into the dark stone walls and found herself in her room without even knowing how she had reached it. She flung herself down on her bed and buried her hot face in her pillow. Life was getting ever more complicated.

CHAPTER SEVEN

DINNER that evening was a somewhat strained occasion. The Contessa did her best to keep up a bright, friendly conversation, but she had little help from the other members of the party around the long table. Even Hector MacDonald was subdued, although he did exclaim pleasurably over the main course of the meal, a particularly delicious concoction of veal, mushrooms, cheese and tomato in a delicately creamy sauce. His daughter, however, was almost totally silent except when she replied monosyllabically to something the Contessa said to her.

Piero was silent, too. He looked pale, thought Amanda, staring at him. Was he as anxious as herself to seize the opportunity for a quiet talk? Their engagement was beginning to be an embarrassment to both of them, it seemed, but she suspected that Piero was not yet aware of her own altered feelings, and was nervous about breaking to her the truth about his own true wishes.

Whenever his glance met that of Magdalen, Amanda caught once more that shadowy unhappiness she had first seen when they arrived. It grew increasingly obvious that Magdalen was in love with Piero. But Piero's feelings towards her were not so clear.

At the head of the table Cesare sat, sardonic and watchful, saying little but seeing everything.

Amanda tried to resist the temptation of looking at .

him, but her eyes irresistibly flickered towards him every
few moments. He was far too good-looking, she thought
wistfully, and possessed the sort of animal magnetism one
usually saw in some sleek black panther, padding stealth-
ily through lush undergrowth in the jungle, his eyes
gleaming with menace. The image made her giggle. She
hurriedly stifled the sound, looking down at her plate.
When she looked up, Cesare was staring at her, brows
drawn. She could not help dimpling, remembering the
black panther, and his frown darkened. She realised then
that he thought she was making fun of him, and she
looked away in haste.

Magdalen asked her politely how it felt to be back in
San Volenco after a long absence.

'I felt at home again within five minutes,' she admitted.

'You are at home,' chided the Contessa fondly.

'And you will never leave us again,' added Aunt
Teresa with a happy sigh.

Cesare leaned back, watching her. Amanda could not
help glancing at him again, despite her wish to keep her
eyes resolutely elsewhere. There was a sardonic gleam in
the grey eyes.

'Aunt Teresa, you are offering Amanda a life sentence,'
he drawled.

Aunt Teresa looked aghast. 'What do you mean?
Manda loves us all. She will be Piero's wife...'

'Will she?' Cesare murmured drily.

A peculiar, taut silence succeeded his question.

Amanda sat with burning cheeks, avoiding everyone's eyes.

'What is that supposed to mean?' asked Piero abruptly.

'What do you think?' Cesare retorted.

'Cesare!' the Contessa murmured in distress.

Aunt Teresa gave a little moan and rose from the table, plunging for the door.

Hector MacDonald coughed loudly and looked around the table in embarrassment. His daughter, however, was looking from Cesare to Piero with great interest, leaning forward to watch them both, her face even paler than usual.

'Make yourself quite clear, please,' Piero said tersely.

Cesare laughed mockingly. 'My pompous little brother! Why are the young always so pompous?'

'I am not being pompous,' Piero said angrily. 'I merely want to know why you implied that Amanda would not be my wife?'

'We have guests, remember,' Cesare said lightly. 'This cannot be very pleasant for them. I suggest we postpone the discussion until a more fitting occasion.'

'You began it,' Piero pointed out furiously. 'Did you expect me to ignore your remark?'

'I expect you to have some common sense,' Cesare said. 'Magdalen may require some coffee. You have not offered to pour her a second cup . . .'

'Don't mind me,' said Magdalen. 'I'm fascinated. Carry on with your frank discussions by all means.'

Piero looked at her, his handsome young face very

pale, his eyes almost imploring.

'Magdalen!'

She gazed at him thoughtfully. Amanda, watching, thought she detected a sort of scorn in the other girl's large almond eyes. 'It's interesting to know that even a Druetso is not automatically suitable as a bride!' There was sarcasm and bitterness in her light voice.

'Cesare did not mean that,' said Piero.

'So you do know what I meant,' murmured his brother drily.

Piero glared at him. 'Oh, I know! But I want you to have to say it out loud, dear brother! I want to hear the high and mighty master of San Volenco admit that I have managed to capture something he is desperate to possess . . .'

Cesare thrust back his chair, his dark face almost white with rage. His eyes flashed with fury as he stared at his brother. The Contessa stood up, too, trembling slightly. She stepped between them and looked at Piero angrily.

'My son, that was unforgivable. How dare you speak of our dearest Amanda as if she was an object like a chair or a table?'

Piero had the grace to flush and look ashamed. 'I am sorry . . .'

'I should think so! But it is to Amanda that you must say you are sorry, not to me!'

Piero glanced briefly in Amanda's direction. 'I apologise, Amanda.'

Hector MacDonald said uneasily, 'Hey, maybe it would be better if we left you two alone for a while,

Piero? You and your brother obviously have a problem, and my old mother always used to say that families should talk out their problems together and not let them fester inside themselves.'

'There is no problem,' Piero said flatly.

'No?' Cesare asked him pointedly.

The younger man looked back at him coldly. 'I don't see one, myself. I am going to marry Amanda, that is all . . .'

'Then that seems to be that,' Magdalen said in a brittle, forced voice.

Amanda was thrown into bewilderment by Piero's flat statement. There was a triumphant, almost menacing air about him as he rose and moved to leave the room. For the first time she really thought hard about Piero and his motive in asking her to marry him. She had believed at first that he was genuinely in love with her, then she had begun to doubt her own feelings towards him, after which she had begun to doubt his love for her, especially since she had seen him with Magdalen. For a short while she had been sure he would be glad to be released from his engagement so that he might, perhaps, marry the beautiful American girl who quite obviously loved him. Now Amanda was thrown into confusion again. What was Piero really playing at? What were his true feelings?

She followed him hurriedly and caught at his sleeve. 'Piero, we must talk . . .'

He looked at her reluctantly. 'Oh, Amanda . . . now?'

'Now is as good a time as any,' she insisted.

He shrugged. 'Very well. Where?'

'Somewhere private, obviously,' she said. 'We must be alone without witnesses.'

He sighed. 'I suppose so.'

'There's been too much public discussion of our affairs already, Piero,' she said bluntly.

He flushed. 'I know. I'm sorry—I lost my temper.'

'You should have been more discreet.'

'If you had lived under Cesare's shadow for so long you would have lost your patience, too,' he exclaimed.

'No doubt I would,' she agreed, not without sympathy. 'But not in front of so many people.'

Piero groaned. 'All right, don't rub it in. I should have held my tongue. Where shall I see you?'

'The walled garden?'

He nodded. 'In ten minutes.'

She grimaced. 'And let's hope Cesare is too busy to go up to his room and hurl flowerpots at us from his balcony!'

'There you are,' said Piero. 'He might have killed us!'

'I think he aimed to one side,' she said.

'He has a shocking temper, all the same,' Piero said. Then he gave a little grin. 'And he was insane with jealousy, of course, seeing you in my arms...'

Amanda felt the colour rush into her cheeks, and she turned away without answering.

It was quite dark when she slipped into the walled garden and closed the door behind her. The air was still warm from the heat of the sun, the fragrance of the flowers still hung heavily upon the stone walls, but the birds were all silent now, and as she stood in the darkness, listening for Piero, the only sound she heard was the distant murmur of voices from down in the city, a sound rather akin to the far-off sound of the sea in a shell when it is held to the ear.

A few stars were out, brightening the velvety blackness of the sky like jewels pinned upon a piece of black velvet, and from behind a cloud a slow radiance spread across the night as the moon came up.

Piero opened the door, closed it and stood there, getting used to the darkness after the electric light within.

'I'm here,' she whispered.

He joined her quietly.

'Well, Piero?' she asked him. 'We have a lot to say to each other, I think.'

He sighed. 'I'm aware of the fact that I ought to apologise. Don't think I am not conscious of being a heel...'

'Why did you ask me to marry you?' she asked curiously.

He groaned. 'You get right to the point, don't you, *cara*?'

'You were not in love with me,' she stated calmly.

Piero shrugged. 'How can I explain? I wasn't ... and yet ... I was...'

'Oh, come on!'

'Don't be angry, Amanda *mia*,' he pleaded. 'Look, let me tell you the story in my own way. You'll understand better.'

'Very well,' she agreed. 'Go ahead.'

'Well,' he said, urging her to sit down on the little

bench behind them, 'it all began, I suppose with Magdalen...'

'I knew she came into it somewhere!'

'I suppose we were pretty transparent,' he sighed.

'I wouldn't say that,' Amanda said, affectionately. 'I do know you pretty well, Piero, and Magdalen didn't bother to hide how she felt.'

He was silent for a moment, then he said warmly, 'You are a nice girl, Amanda. You know that? I do love you, believe me, in a way...'

'Like a brother!' Amanda said sarcastically.

He grimaced. 'I deserved that!'

'Oh, get on with your story!'

'The MacDonalds came here to look round the stables because they were interested in buying some bloodstock from us, and they became great friends with us all. I found Magdalen very attractive, and we dated for a while. I was on the point of asking her to marry me ... well, I'd hinted at the idea once or twice, and she was not discouraging, but you know how it is when you're young. I wasn't in a hurry to tie myself down then and there. But before I had actually popped the question her father dropped a bombshell...'

'He bought the Mireze stables!'

'Oh, you know! Yes, that was it, and Cesare swore eternal enmity towards the whole MacDonald clan. Well, I wasn't too pleased, myself. After all, it was a bit of a foul trick to play—he knew Cesare wanted Mireze. But I still intended to marry Magdalen—even though

Cesare made it clear he would be dead set against any such idea.'

'So what went wrong?'

'Well, first of all, Hector more or less insulted me.' Piero's voice grew fierce. 'He offered me a job at Mireze at a higher salary. I saw it as a bribe and turned him down. Magdalen was annoyed with me. She had suggested it to him as a way out of the difficulty. She didn't want to come and live at Volenco, she said. She didn't like the feudal atmosphere.'

'I know what she means!'

'Well, we had a big row about it. I didn't see her for a while. Cesare had forbidden me to bring her to Volenco again, anyway, and to get me away from her he sent me to England.'

'Where you met me,' Amanda prompted.

'Yes.' He sighed.

'Be honest, Piero. What did you hope to achieve by dating me and asking me to marry you?'

'I dated you because I was pleased to see you,' he protested. 'We could speak Italian together. You were a familiar face. I've always been fond of you.'

'It was you who made the running, though, Piero ... You changed our brother-and-sister relationship deliberately!'

'You're an attractive girl. Was that so strange?'

'Oh, Piero!'

He took her hand in his and stroked it gently. 'I'm trying to be honest, *cara*. It is true, you see—I found you very attractive. You're a beautiful girl.'

'And Cesare had nothing to do with it?' she probed.

'Who can say that their motives are easy to explain? I admit that I was partly motivated by a desire to make love to the girl who had rejected my brother! I was fascinated by the idea, to be absolutely honest. You were beautiful, and you were the only female I had ever met who had given my wonderful, all-powerful brother a good kick in the teeth. How could I resist the temptation to see if I could win a battle he had publicly lost?'

'It was unworthy of you,' she protested.

'I'm human,' he said, a little sulkily, and Amanda realised how much of a little boy there was in his character.

'And when you asked me to marry you? Did you sincerely mean to go through with it?'

'Of course I did,' he said, almost indignantly. 'By then I was sure I was truly in love. You were exciting to make love to . . .'

'Because each time you kissed me you were getting your own back on Cesare?' she said sarcastically.

'Don't undervalue yourself,' said Piero. 'Quite apart from my desire to hurt Cesare, I was easily able to fancy you.'

'Thanks,' she said. 'That certainly helps my ego!' Her voice had a bitter ring which made him shift uneasily. 'You weren't in love with me,' he said uncertainly.

'Wasn't I?' Scorn filled her voice.

Piero tried to see her face in the darkness, but could only catch the glitter of her uplifted eyes. 'Were you?' His voice had grown humble now.

'No,' she said tersely. 'As it happens, I wasn't, but you couldn't have known that when you began your little game. You talk very prettily about finding me attractive, Piero, but the rock-bottom truth is that your motive was almost entirely one of revenge, a particularly spiteful revenge on your brother for having exerted some sort of authority over you.'

'Authority?' Piero sounded furious. 'He is what you said he was ... a tyrant! The Tyrant of San Volenco! He has always treated me as an inferior. It was Cesare who made the decisions, Cesare who laid down the law, Cesare who ran things. I was the underling, the junior ... I had to learn to smile and be charming to him ... any sort of rebellion was fatal.'

'You mean you couldn't meet him on his own terms. He was too strong for you.'

'He's an arrogant bastard! He always has been!'

'You should have asserted yourself earlier instead of relying on this sort of spiteful trick to get your own back ...'

Piero jumped to his feet. 'Stop lecturing me! I've had enough of that from Magdalen.'

'Ah, yes, Magdalen. We're back to her. How did you come to see her again?'

'She heard that I was going to the Florence conference, and she rang me at the vineyard one day, and invited me to stay with them in their Florence house. They live there part of the year and part of the year at Mireze.'

'Didn't she know you were engaged?' asked Amanda, somewhat surprised at this news.

'She knew,' Piero said grimly. 'She wanted to ask me why, and to hear about you from me myself ... She had only heard gossip of the usual sort from neighbours and friends. She knew you were a distant member of the family. She had heard about you long ago. But she had not expected an engagement between us.'

'Naturally not,' said Amanda drily.

He grimaced. 'Don't think I wasn't sick with myself. I was ... and after I'd heard her voice again I felt worse. My feelings for her came alive again.'

'Inconvenient,' Amanda commented.

'Don't make fun of me! I was miserable! I thought I ought to see her once more, explain how I had come to get engaged to you ... break off all relations with her family.'

'And I talked you into going there!'

'Yes. Cesare, of course, didn't tell you why he had forbidden me to see her again.'

'Cesare had more scruples than you did, apparently,' Amanda said. 'He never hinted to me once that there had been anyone else in your life.'

'Scruples? Do you expect me to believe Cesare was being scrupulous? It is far more likely that he was saving Magdalen as ammunition for later in his campaign.'

'His campaign?' Amanda froze.

Piero sat down beside her again and took her hand in his, rubbing her cold fingers. 'I've been honest with you, be the same with me. Cesare has not neglected his opportunity, has he? He has tried to get you to change your mind?'

'Why should you think so?'

'Because he warned me before I left that he would do precisely that,' said Piero irritably.

'Oh,' she breathed. 'He warned you, did he?'

'Cesare is like that,' Piero said flatly. 'He is a bastard, as I said, but he is a just bastard. He told me that he considered I'd had no right to steal you away from him. He has always thought of you as his property, you must know that.'

'I didn't know,' Amanda said breathlessly.

'I can't believe that! Why, even when you were a little girl he was fascinated by you and your likeness to the Beatrice portrait. He carried you everywhere with him. He hated to have you out of his sight. We all knew that when you were old enough he would marry you. He could never keep his eyes off you for a second. He was always running his fingers through your long hair, watching you, talking about you ... Cesare's great weakness, we all thought you ... his Achilles heel.'

'You knew this and you never so much as hinted at it to me when we met again in England?'

'You had refused him,' Piero pointed out. 'You had stayed away for five years! I did not think you cared.'

'But you knew Cesare still cared?' she accused. 'You wanted to bring me back here to San Volenco because you were sure it would be the thing most calculated to hurt him! I was the instrument of your revenge, wasn't I, Piero? You used me!'

'What if I did?' he demanded angrily. 'Because of Cesare my own love affair had been smashed to pieces!

Why shouldn't he be hurt in his turn? I don't mind admitting it. I wanted to see him wince. I couldn't wait to see his face. His jealousy was the sweetest balm I could have asked for . . .'

'Your own brother! How could you?'

'Amanda, have you forgotten your advice to me only a short while ago? You told me then that Cesare was a dictator and advised me to rebel against him. Now you turn on me accusingly for doing just that!'

'You didn't have to torture him!'

Piero laughed bitterly. 'Didn't I? What other course was open to me? Cesare has never listened to reason. He has always treated me scornfully—I'm his kid brother, the idiot whose role in life has always been to do what Cesare tells me. He would never have taken me seriously. He is taking me seriously now, though. He started taking me seriously when I brought you home as my future wife.'

Amanda stared up at his dark face, taken aback by what he had just told her. She knew how much truth there was in it—Cesare had always been inclined to ride rough-shod over people, especially over Piero. She sighed.

'I suppose I see your point. I only wish you hadn't used me in your scheme . . .'

'I'm sorry, Amanda, I'm truly sorry. At the time I thought I loved you enough to be very happy with you. It wasn't just a plot. I genuinely found you attractive from the start . . .'

'Never mind me. I'm sorry for Magdalen. She will never be able to trust you.'

'Do you think I don't know that?' There was real pain in his voice. 'She's already told me as much. I'm afraid Magdalen is angry and bitter about the whole thing.'

'I noticed,' said Amanda drily. 'Are you surprised?'

'It has hardly been entirely my fault,' he complained.

Piero was very immature, Amanda realised, listening to him as he continued to talk about Magdalen. He was always looking for a scapegoat for his own shortcomings, unable to admit that he might personally be to blame. His attitude was not uncommon, but he had not learned to disguise it. He was still quite childishly open about it, indeed.

'When you tell her that we have broken off our engagement, it may improve things between you,' she said, cutting him short.

'Is our engagement at an end?' Piero asked flatly.

She was astounded. 'But of course! How can you ask after what we have just been discussing?'

Piero mumbled something, then said, 'I suppose you hate me, too, now? Like Magdalen, you blame me for this mess...'

'Who else can I blame?' she asked him, then laughed abruptly. 'Well, myself, of course! I should have known. I think I did, from the start, but I stifled my misgivings for my own twisted reasons. We all have hidden motives, don't we, Piero? And how many of us really understand why we do things? We think up such excellent excuses for ourselves, we rationalise what we know to be irrational, and we always prefer to blame someone else when we make a stupid mistake.'

Piero sounded puzzled. 'I'm sorry, Amanda. Will you forgive me one day?' He gave a little snort of cross amusement. 'One day soon, no doubt, you will be my sister-in-law.'

'I shouldn't lay bets on it,' she said crisply.

'Oh, I think I would,' Piero said cynically.

'I shall not be marrying Cesare,' she insisted.

'Amanda, *cara*! Cesare means to marry you, whatever you think! I tell you, my dear brother is insanely in love with you ... even I underestimated how he felt about you. He will not take no for an answer this time.'

'He'll have to!'

'No,' Piero murmured. 'You forget that the hawk never gives up his prey. Once he has swooped, there is no escape.'

CHAPTER EIGHT

Next morning Signora Marella returned to show Amanda her altered costume. It was still delicately styled, flimsy and fluttering, but it had been cleverly remodelled to be less revealing. Amanda was far less embarrassed when she tried it on this time, and she warmly congratulated the Signora on her work.

'It is very well done, Signora! Thank you.'

'And now you will not be afraid to appear in the procession, Manda?' The Signora was pleased with her appreciation. She liked to feel that her work was well received.

'I shall still be nervous, but at least I shall not be totally petrified,' Amanda admitted.

The Signora smiled approvingly at her. 'You are naturally modest. That is as it should be ... not like that Tina, who is a shameless creature...'

'She sees a great deal of Giulio,' Amanda murmured. 'Perhaps she will marry him?'

'Why should Giulio marry her?' The Signora was scornful. 'A man does not buy the cake after he has had a slice!'

Amanda flushed, gasping. 'Oh!'

Signora Marella gave her an indulgent glance. 'You are very naïve, *cara*, if you did not realise how it is between them ... and you have lived in London!'

'London is not the sinful city you imagine, perhaps,' Amanda laughed.

Signora Marella grinned. 'No, I think we have as much sin here in Volenco as anywhere else!'

'What an admission!' drawled a voice from the door.

Amanda's pulses quickened as she turned. Cesare met her gaze coolly. He had changed his jodhpurs for a formal dark suit and crisp white tie, and looked devastatingly handsome.

His eyes moved slowly over her. 'Yes,' he said, nodding. 'That looks much better. It may send up the temperatures of a few young men, but it won't actually start a riot!'

Amanda slipped quickly behind the screen to change back into her ordinary clothes. She heard Signora Marella talking to Cesare, then the door closed quietly. He had gone! With a sigh of relief she emerged from behind the screen, but it was Signora Marella who had gone. Cesare remained behind, leaning against the window frame, his dark face inscrutable.

She felt hot colour sting her cheeks. Their eyes clashed and hers fell.

'We barely exchanged two words during our ride this morning,' Cesare drawled. 'Isn't it time you told me what you have decided to do?'

'Do? About what?' She pretended confusion.

His mouth tightened. 'You know perfectly well what I'm talking about. What have you decided to do about this mock engagement of yours? Have you given Piero his marching orders?'

'I refuse to discuss my private affairs with you,' she said coldly, moving to the door.

Cesare moved swiftly, blocking her path. He was expressionless, yet she sensed a dark emotion emanating from him, and shrank back, trembling.

'How much longer do you expect me to put up with this?' he asked her thickly. 'I'm not made of steel. After yesterday you must have a pretty good idea of Piero's motives. Why don't you put a stop to this idiocy once and for all?'

She was about to answer when the door opened quietly behind his shoulder, and he was forced to move out of the way. Magdalen MacDonald came into the room, looking enquiringly from one to the other of them.

'Oh, I'm sorry . . . am I interrupting something?'

The words made Amanda blush. She shook her head hurriedly, trying to smile. 'Of course not! Come in . . . this is the old medieval solar, you know. It was the private sitting-room of the Count and his wife in the days when everyone lived together down in the great hall. It's rather cold in winter—these stone walls are damp. But the tapestries help to make it habitable.'

Cesare politely excused himself and left. Amanda half collapsed against a chair with relief, then smiled brightly as her eye met that of Magdalen again.

'He's really something, isn't he?' Magdalen said.

Amanda laughed, but did not reply. She did not know quite how to answer that remark without betraying herself.

'Has anyone ever shown you the tapestries?' she asked,

instead, trying to make the conversation fall into more general categories. 'They were specially made for this room during the seventeenth century. They're secular subjects, as you'll see ... in earlier centuries the artists and embroiderers always used religious subjects, but during the Renaissance, of course, the subject matter was broadened to include other things. It coincided with the religious wars between Catholic and Protestant. Until then the church had controlled art, but after that art was more free to choose its own material, and we get tapestries like this one, with these hunting scenes...'

'Very impressive,' Magdalen said drily. 'But couldn't we talk about Piero? Don't you think we should?'

Amanda glanced at her uneasily. 'Well, no ... I don't, to be quite frank. I think you should talk to him yourself.'

'I've tried, but he's avoiding me.'

'This morning?'

'Just now,' Magdalen nodded. 'He saw me coming towards him in the garden and scooted like a frightened deer.'

Amanda frowned. 'I wonder why?'

'You tell me,' Magdalen invited.

'I don't know.' Amanda met her incredulous gaze and repeated. 'I don't know—honestly! I thought he would say something to you today.'

Magdalen lifted her eyes to the tapestry beside her. It was silvery grey and sage green, the colours muted by time until they were barely distinguishable. The fleeing deer were pale shadows. The hunters, in beautifully drawn pursuit, were worn and faded, their tunics rusty with age and dust.

'Why is that bird hovering overhead like that?' Magdalen said. 'And why does he wear a ribbon round his neck?'

Amanda looked at the tapestry reluctantly. She knew what she would see. Her skin chilled as she looked at it. 'That's a hawk,' she said quietly. 'It's the emblem of the Counts of Volenco, and the ribbon round its neck carries a jewel, the famous seal of the Count, a huge ruby set in gold and enamel.'

Magdalen studied the hawk thoughtfully. 'Cruel birds, hawks,' she observed. 'Look at those talons!'

Amanda looked away. 'I prefer not to look,' she said, trembling slightly.

Magdalen sat down on a gold-painted, thin-legged little salon chair beside the window. 'You know, I got a new idea of what was going on here from what Piero said last night at the table. I'd have to be pretty dumb not to know that you were more Cesare's girl than Piero's.'

Amanda flushed hotly. 'Piero had no business to talk like that in front of visitors!'

'We aren't just visitors,' Magdalen said crisply. 'I'll put my cards on the table. I love Piero, and I believe he loves me. The only stumbling block in our path is his family. Cesare doesn't want anything to do with us for two reasons. One: my father got in first at Mireze. Two: we're Americans, and Cesare isn't too keen on Americans. Oh, he's polite! But the hostility is there underneath all the time.'

'I think the hostility is mainly caused because of Mireze,' Amanda denied quickly. 'After all, you knew very well that Cesare wanted it!'

'Of course we knew,' Magdalen said easily. 'But we didn't ever suspect Cesare would be angry!'

'But surely?' Amanda stared at her. 'You must have guessed how he would feel! Anyone would be angry in those circumstances. You deliberately bought the place which Cesare had always longed to own! He would have to be a saint to forgive you!'

Magdalen stared at her earnestly. 'But don't you see ... we bought Mireze for Piero!'

Amanda was stunned. 'You ... did what?'

'It was going to belong to a Druetso, anyway,' Magdalen explained. 'Dad was going to give it to Piero and me after we were married. He would have lived in Florence most of the time. It would have been Piero and me at Mireze.'

'Oh!' Amanda breathed, understanding.

'It was all meant to be a wonderful surprise,' Magdalen went on. 'We never dreamt Cesare would be so mad, or that Piero would behave like a craven idiot, and break off with me like that ... Everything went wrong. It was made pretty clear to us that only a Druetso could own a place like Mireze. We were aliens, interlopers. We weren't welcome around here any more.'

'Good heavens,' Amanda said, in sympathy. 'It must have been a shock to you!'

'It was hell,' Magdalen admitted huskily.

'You love Piero?'

Magdalen shrugged. 'I did love him, yes.'

'Did?' Amanda stared at her shrewdly. 'Now you have doubts about it?'

'Is that surprising after the way he's behaved? Letting his brother order him around like that, breaking off with me, going off to England, and then to crown it all, coming back with a fiancée!'

'I don't blame you for having doubts,' Amanda agreed. 'And it will do Piero good to have to work to win you back. He's far too self-indulgent.'

Magdalen gazed at her thoughtfully. 'You don't love him, do you?'

'No,' Amanda agreed.

'It's Cesare for you?'

Amanda turned away. 'There's no one for me,' she said abruptly, biting her lip.

The city began to fill up with tourists as the day of the Beatrice pageant approached. The few hotels were already fully booked. The city council were constantly on the alert for signs of anyone attempting to camp out in the streets—numbers of hippies had to be turfed out of the city each evening when they tried to bed down in a dark corner in scruffy sleeping bags.

The weather remained warm and fine, fortunately. A threatened storm moved away in another direction when the wind changed, and the day of the pageant dawned bright and clear.

Amanda lifted her head, yawning, as her alarm clock went off with a shrill clatter. She did not feel much like getting up. They had gone to bed late last night—there were so many last-minute arrangements to make. The whole business had proved unbelievably complicated. She never wished to help to organise such a thing again; so many small details could go wrong.

She was standing in the middle of her room, stretching, when the door opened and Cesare stood there.

She straightened up hastily, blushing. 'Really, Cesare! Why the hell don't you knock? It's embarrassing to have a man walking in and out of one's room without knocking ... I might have been getting dressed!'

He mockingly flicked a glance over her. 'You look very neat, but I'm afraid you won't be needing your jodhpurs. There will not be a ride this morning. I forgot to mention it last night. There will be too many coaches down on the roads ... too much traffic everywhere ... The horses will have to skip their exercise for today.'

'They won't like that,' she smiled.

'No.' He shrugged. 'It can't be helped.'

They had hardly been alone since Magdalen arrived. She had joined them on their morning rides each day. Amanda had been grateful for her company—it had avoided the opportunity of any intimate talk with Cesare. Fortunately he had been so busy with the pageant organisation that he had had little time to spare for anything else.

She stood now, waiting for him to leave, her head nervously lowered. The fine golden curls clung to her neck. One had fallen down into the V of her white shirt.

Cesare leant forward and gently lifted it out, and she started back, alarmed.

'No need to scream,' he said sarcastically. 'I'm not intending rape. I'm too busy this morning.'

'Well, thank goodness for that,' she said crossly.

He laughed. 'But one of these days, Amanda ... one of these days ...'

He was gone on the words, the door closing quietly behind him. Amanda pressed her hands to her hot cheeks and wished her pulses would not race so fast at the sight of him.

The procession was to gather in the great hall before the moment for the doors to be flung open and their long winding line to pass out into the streets. This was due to take place precisely at eleven o'clock.

At ten, therefore, Amanda was in her bedroom again, after a light breakfast she had not wanted at all but which the Contessa had insisted on forcing her to eat. Slowly, with trembling fingers, she put on her costume and then inspected herself in the mirror.

'I can't do it,' she moaned to herself. 'I can't go out there in front of all those people like this ...'

Again she surveyed the fluttering wisps of gauze, the wreath of flowers on her hair, the tiny gold sandals which made an audacious pretence of being useful.

She remembered her meeting with Piero in London—the silver fairground horse, the merry-go-round, the flashing lights and the bright tawdry of the fair. She had the same dizzy, incredulous feeling now. She was being whirled around in space and time, helpless to intervene on her own behalf, feeling confused and weak as everything flashed past her eyes.

Signora Marella bustled into the room, stopped to survey her with shrewd eyes.

'*Bellissima*,' she nodded. 'That is perfect! Now you look just like the Beatrice! You will become famous! Have you seen the city this morning? So many photographers ... journalists ... everywhere there are newspapermen! Even the television cameras have arrived.'

Amanda felt faint. 'No!' Horror weakened her legs beneath her. She covered her face with her hands. 'I can't do it ... I won't go out there ... cameras and photographers ... it's terrifying!'

'It will be exciting! You'll see, you will love it once it starts ... your picture in all the newspapers, seeing yourself on the television ...'

'How ghastly!' Amanda moaned. 'I would hate it, don't you understand that?'

Signora Marella did not understand that at all. She envied Amanda her chance of fame. Bewildered, she said, 'You have not thought about it! The fuss they will make of you! You will be famous all over the world.'

The door opened. Cesare came in, wearing a Renaissance costume that made Signora Marella gasp in surprise and admiration. He was magnificent in black and silver. His sleeves were full and ballooned to the wrist, tied at intervals all the way along, with silver ribbons. His fifteenth-century pleated tunic was black silk trimmed with silver, his stockings matched. On his head he wore a feather-trimmed black velvet cap.

He gestured to Signora Marella to leave, and she quickly obeyed him. Cesare leaned against the closed door, staring across the room at Amanda.

'You look very handsome,' she said shakily. 'I didn't know you were going to dress up, too.'

'Don't you recognise me?' he asked lightly.

She stared at him for a long moment, then hot colour burned in her cheeks as she realised that he was meant to resemble Beatrice's husband, the Hawk of Volenco. There was a small portrait of him in similar clothes, although it needed cleaning badly, and was not as compellingly painted as the Botticelli portrait of his wife. Some more pedestrian painter had been brought in to do a painting of him later, perhaps.

'Why not a centaur's costume?' she asked bitterly.

Cesare looked amused. 'What a wasp-tongued little girl you can be at times! You must not sting me, though. I sting back.'

'I'm sure you do! Well, you can find someone else to play Beatrice! I can't do it.'

Cesare shot her a cool look. 'Why not?'

'I'm terrified,' she cried, shaking. 'Can't you see? It must be as plain as the nose on your face that I'm in no condition to go out into the streets and make a show of myself!'

'Stage-fright,' he diagnosed calmly. 'Everyone else is feeling the same, don't worry.'

Amanda was taken aback, and stared at him in disbelief. 'Everyone else is feeling the same? Do you mean that?'

'Of course I do. Do you imagine you have got the monopoly of last-minute nerves? I've just been into the main dressing-room and found it full of women in the last stages of sheer unadulterated panic ... it was like walking into a hen-coop after they've sighted the fox! I was instantly seized around the neck by two squawking women and half strangled to death. I only escaped with my life because I had had the foresight to take a bottle of brandy with me. I left them all sipping doubtfully at a glass.'

She giggled, the picture swamping all other feelings. 'I'm sure you're exaggerating wildly, but it is a relief to know I'm not the only one with nerves. Signora Marella...'

'Ah, the Signora,' said Cesare thoughtfully. 'She was no doubt making you feel worse by dramatising the number of people waiting outside to see you?'

'She did say there were squads of reporters and TV cameras outside,' Amanda admitted, feeling rather foolish.

Cesare laughed. 'And you believed her? My dear girl!'

'Aren't there?' asked Amanda doubtfully.

'A few, perhaps—hardly squads! Look, *cara*, this is just a game, some fun we have ... it is an amusement! Not a subtle form of torture!' He moved nearer, smiling down at her. He was broad and lithe in the magnificent costume. The black and silver suited him, gave him a sort of sombre grandeur which exactly matched his dark hair and cruelly handsome Renaissance face. Just so must his ancestor have looked to Beatrice as she fled him, looking back with wide, panic-stricken eyes over her naked shoulder.

She breathed a sigh of relief. 'Oh, well, I feel better now I know that.'

'I am glad,' he said softly. His long brown hand came out to capture her chin, lift it so that her eyes met his in a silent glance.

'You look enchanting,' he told her. She was suddenly deeply, savagely aware of his nearness, and her body shook with the impact of a realisation which terrified her. She loved this man. She wanted him with a passion as intense as that which she knew he felt for her. Yet her mind, cool and clear above the turmoil of her emotions, told her that it was mere folly to give in to her desire. Cesare would never make her happy. Surrender to him would be a surrender of all independence, all free will. She would become his chattel, the possession of his pleasure.

Amanda's pride would not permit her to sacrifice her whole freedom in exchange for the delights of satisfied desire.

'Thank you,' she told him coolly, moving backwards so that he had to release her.

For a moment he hesitated, and she tensed, waiting for the inevitable struggle between them, but Cesare seemed to think better of it. He shrugged, making a little grimace of the lips.

'Now, you will not be nervous,' he said instead. 'You will enjoy yourself. Good luck. Remember, you are very beautiful, *cara*. Every man in the crowd will admire you.'

She flushed. The idea was still nerve-racking. She did not want to be admired. Being in the public eye was unbearable. But she had to go through with it now. There was no turning back; it was too late.

With Cesare's dark presence at her side she made her way down to the hall to join the others. Cesare had only to glance at her to reassure her. She felt his strength like the walls of the old castle around her. He protected, uplifted her, wrapped her round with care and love.

Tina was watching her as she looked around the hall. Amanda met Tina's eyes nervously, feeling the other girl's hatred and anger as if it were a physical thing. She knew instinctively that Tina resented the fact that Cesare stood beside her, protecting her. Tina coveted Cesare. Amanda knew that Tina did not love him. There was no softness in the other girl's stare, only a blatant physical hunger which she did nothing to disguise. Amanda shivered and turned away. She hated the thought of them together ... Jealousy burnt inside her as she saw Cesare smile at Tina.

Giulio was there, talking to the Contessa. He was looking at one of the old blood-red glass goblets which the Contessa cherished so reverently. Amanda frowned, seeing Giulio stroke it lovingly. Surely the Contessa was not going to sell her old Venetian glass? It was very valuable, and had been in the family for many years. Amanda wondered if Cesare was aware that his mother was selling things. Was she doing it without his knowledge? And why was she having to sell things? Amanda had been back long enough to have discovered that, in the main, the Volenco estates were doing very well. Of course, Cesare always complained about not having enough money, but in fact it was clear that he was very comfortably off. The estate was making more money than it used to—it was far more efficiently run and was growing more productive every year.

She had no time to mention the Venetian glass to Cesare, however, for the time had come. The great Cathedral bell began to ring, high above them. Cesare smiled at her, and the procession shuffled hurriedly into a more precise line.

They had rehearsed it so many times, but now that the great day had arrived they all fell into a momentary state of panic.

Voices babbled helplessly. People pushed and argued. The line wobbled, then straightened out again. Cesare moved away from Amanda to take command. At the cool sound of his voice the disorder disappeared as rapidly as it had begun. Everyone grew calm. People smiled and fell into place. The doors were flung open and into the shadowy hall streamed the golden Italian sunshine.

The head of the procession moved out, as arranged. First marched the city trumpeters, in traditional short velvet tunics, emblazoned with gold. They blew a fanfare, then moved ahead. Behind them came the drummers, three boys from the city below, deftly beating a tattoo upon their drums as they marched behind the trumpeters. Their livery matched that of the trumpeters, and bore the city arms emblazoned on their chests.

The flag-bearers came next, twirling the six flags of the city districts. Despite the small size of San Volenco it had always been divided into districts. There were the four quarters; the east, the west, the south, the north. Then there were the so-called New, or Gate, district and the Castle District. Each had always had its own device. The Gate and Castle devices were obvious. Then there were the Eagle, the Stag, the Hound and the Fountain devices. They made colourful displays as they swung the flags to and fro above their heads. The bright silks fluttered gaily in the sunshine. The east district had chosen the Fountain device because it had once held the chief source of water, and it was proud of this distinction even though today the water was piped into the city from a central reservoir instead of coming from the ancient city springs.

Behind the flags came the procession. The rich costumes and smiling faces attracted ripples of applause. Tina preened herself delightedly as she received an outburst of excited clapping. Amanda, who was to bring up the rear, trembled violently as she waited to move out. Her nerves were almost on the point of collapse.

Cesare moved to her side. He took her cold, shaking fingers and pressed them gently. 'Don't be afraid, my darling!'

She tried to smile. 'I won't,' she promised faintly.

Then the moment was upon her, and she forced her shaking limbs to move. The brilliance of the light, the heat, the noise, dazzled and blinded her. She moved forward in a trance, her dazed eyes seeing nothing but the back of the girl in front. A slight breeze rustled the flimsy draperies she wore. Her skin was delicately, translucently pale. Her golden ringlets blew back from her face, exposing the fragility of her slender throat, emphasising the fine bone structure, the matt smoothness of her skin.

The crowd stared, falling silent. Their cries and clapping gave way to an almost reverent fascination. Many of them had seen the Botticelli painting she resembled so much. Cheap copies of it were, indeed, being sold in every souvenir shop in the city. It was hung up in every window. Even the crude methods of modern reproduction could not blur or totally destroy the exquisite spirituality of the picture, and Amanda was the very living image of it.

Unaware of all this, she walked with sleep-walking concentration behind the others, looking neither to left nor to right, uncaring that she was filling the crowd with awe, uncaring that she outshone every other person in the procession.

All she wanted was to get to the end of this torture, to hide herself once more in the shadows of the castle, away from all these staring eyes.

They made the arranged tour of the streets. Gradually the crowd lost its awe of Amanda, and began to applaud her violently, calling out compliments and showering her with flower petals. Geranium petals of every colour clung to her dress and hair. She felt as if she walked in a rain of colour. The strong scent of geranium clung to her insistently.

At last, after what seemed eternity, they were back in

the castle. The light, the noise, the crowds vanished. The procession broke up and began to chatter excitedly. Amanda stood quite still, shivering.

'You looked marvellous,' Magdalen said at her side. Then, in a worried voice, 'Say, are you all right?'

Amanda hardly noticed her. She was trying not to fall forward into the darkness which was awaiting her. Then she sighed and let go, and the darkness rushed up to greet her.

CHAPTER NINE

'STUPID little fool,' murmured Cesare's voice caressingly in her ear as she slowly fought her way back to full consciousness. Amanda stirred, a faint moan on her lips. Her lids fluttered, but they were still too heavy to be lifted.

'I have sent for a doctor,' the Contessa said somewhere close at hand. 'He is coming . . .'

'No need,' said Cesare. 'She is waking up now.'

Reluctantly, Amanda lifted those heavy lids. The light was dazzling. She screwed up her eyes, then closed them again with another moan of protest.

'There,' Cesare said. 'You see? Nothing wrong with her that a quiet hour on her bed won't cure. Draw the curtains. We'll leave her to sleep.'

'I do not think she should be left alone,' the Contessa protested gently.

'Then I will stay with her,' Cesare said firmly.

There was a little silence. Then the Contessa said, 'Perhaps it might be better if I stayed with her, Cesare.'

'As you wish,' Cesare dismissed without argument.

Amanda heard movements, the swish of the curtains being drawn, the trickle of water into a china bowl, then footsteps close beside her. A damp cloth was slowly drawn across her forehead. It was a pleasantly cooling sensation. She was grateful. A smile touched her lips. She

put up one limp hand to touch the fingers which were so
gently soothing her, believing it to be the Contessa, but as
soon as she touched that strong hand she knew it had
been Cesare, and her hand fell away hurriedly.

'We should not have forced her to walk in the procession,' said the Contessa anxiously. 'It was too much of
an ordeal for her. She was always shy and withdrawing.'

Cesare laughed. 'Shy? Amanda? You do not know
her. Modest, yes, and proud. It was her pride which was
outraged today. She hated to be made a public show.'

'We should not have asked it of her!'

'Well, it is over now, and it has been a great triumph.
This year our tourist figures will be treble or quadruple
what they usually are. The Beatrice Pageant will con-
tinue to have an effect for the rest of the season. The
special exhibition of Volenco Portraits will attract tourists for months. Ah, yes, I meant to ask you something—
the Venetian goblets, Mother. Shall we not place them on
exhibition with the other things? They are famous, too. I
would like them to be seen along with the Seal of the
Count, the Renaissance silverware and the family jewel-
lery.'

Amanda opened her eyes, alarmed by Cesare's words.
Her movement, slight though it was, distracted him at
this moment. He turned towards her, looking anxious.

'Did I wake you, *cara*? I am sorry. How do you feel?'

She half sat up. 'Better...'

The Contessa gave her a nervous, gentle smile.
Amanda saw that she was looking worried, and she
wondered again what was going on between the Con-

tessa and Giulio. Now, at least, she knew for certain that Cesare was not in the secret. Whatever it was, the Contessa had not taken him into her confidence.

'Would you like to rest for a while?' Cesare asked her.

Amanda nodded. She glanced at the Contessa. 'Stay with me,' she asked, putting out an appealing hand.

Cesare smiled at them both. 'That is right. You both look pale. I think you both need a time of peace and relaxation. Stay in here during siesta.'

When he had gone, the Contessa relaxed with a sigh. Amanda watched her, trying to think of a way of gaining her confidence without alarming her. She was convinced that something was worrying the Contessa. There was definitely something on her mind. But what?

Tentatively, Amanda asked her, 'Do you like Giulio, Contessa?'

Pink flooded the older woman's pale face. She looked at Amanda with wide eyes, blinking rapidly in a nervous manner. 'Why do you ask?' She tried to laugh as she murmured the words.

'I don't trust him,' Amanda said, gently probing.

The Contessa sighed. 'You are right...'

'Ah, dearest Aunt Maria, tell me what's going on,' Amanda begged in soft Italian. 'I know very well that there's something wrong somewhere. I may be able to help you...'

'No, not you,' the Contessa denied sadly.

Amanda was hurt. 'Not me? But I want to help, truly.'

The Contessa gave a soft croon of affection, kissing her

warmly on the cheek. 'Thank you, *mia cara*. Do you
think I don't know that? You know how dear to me you
are—as dear as my sons! You are the daughter I never
had. You are the child of my dearest Lucia, and the last
thing in the world I desire is for you to be hurt.'

Amanda frowned. 'Hurt? Why should I be hurt?' She
looked at the Contessa sharply. 'Is there some secret involved in this? Is Giulio blackmailing you?'

The Contessa looked startled, biting her pale lip. She
said absolutely nothing, but Amanda's quick intuition
had grown more concrete with every passing second. She
stared at the older woman as if she could read her
thoughts.

'Tell me!' She demanded. 'I'm not a child. Whatever
this secret is it must be brought out into the open. Don't
you know that blackmailers never go away? Like leeches
they cling on, sucking blood from their victims, until
there's nothing left. They're vicious, deadly creatures. I
think blackmail is the worst crime in the book...'

The Contessa covered her face with her hands, col-
lapsing suddenly in total disarray. She moaned something under her breath, but Amanda did not catch it. She
pulled the Contessa into her arms and gently stroked her
hair, murmuring comforting words to her. 'Never mind
... we'll sort it out ... something will be done ...'

The Contessa sat up, kissed her firmly. 'You are right,'
she said. 'I have been a fool. I was so afraid that...' She
bit off the words and tried to smile, pathetically. 'I'm a
silly old woman ...'

'You're not! You're a darling! Never say such things about yourself again!'

The Contessa kissed her gratefully. 'It is such a relief to talk to someone else about it!'

'Giulio is blackmailing you?'

The Contessa nodded. 'He has been for the last two months.'

'The last two months?' Amanda frowned. 'That must have been around the time you heard of my engagement to Piero.'

The Contessa's face again betrayed her. She looked with sad despair at Amanda.

'This secret concerns myself or Piero, then?' Amanda watched her. She caught the very faint flicker of the pale, wrinkled lids. 'Ah, Piero . . . something to do with him?'

The Contessa gazed wildly at her. 'Amanda, I love you, but must you go on like the Spanish Inquisition?' The attempt at humour was brave but unconvincing.

'Tell me, then,' Amanda urged. 'You know you'll feel better!'

The Contessa stared at her, still biting her lips. 'But . . . you don't understand . . . how can I? It was for you that . . .' She broke off the sentence with a choked sob.

Amanda was too quick for her. 'For my sake you gave in to this blackmail? Ah, I see it all now. I'm the last person you want to share this secret with? But, dearest Aunt Maria . . .' She half smiled, half groaned. 'You don't know. You don't realise. Piero and I . . . are finished.' She looked apologetically at the Contessa. 'It was folly from the beginning. We wouldn't have suited.'

The Contessa's eyes searched her face. 'Piero feels this, too?'

'It was always Magdalen for him, I think you know that.'

'Not always,' the Contessa said grimly.

A flash of intuition visited Amanda again. She thought of the intimacy between Giulio and Tina, Tina's hostility towards her, certain cryptic remarks the girl had made Slowly she said, 'Tina and Piero? Is that it?'

The Contessa inclined her head. 'So Giulio claims. He threatened to tell you about it, break up the engagement, if I did not let him sell some of my antiques.'

'But they were priceless!'

'Oh, he gave me a fair price for them,' the Contessa said wryly. 'Giulio is clever—he kept within the law. He sold them in his shop, then he took a fifteen per cent fee from the sum he had earned. The rest he sent to me. It was all legal and above board, except...'

'Except that you didn't want to sell Druetso heir-looms? It's still blackmail and I'm sure he could be prosecuted.'

'Giulio said he would deny my allegations. He said no court would believe me. I had been paid well for the things. What complaint could I make?'

'Oh, Aunt, why did you do it? Cesare is bound to find out, and he'll be so angry! Why didn't you go to him in the beginning, tell him all about Giulio's nasty little scheme? Cesare would have dealt with Giulio pretty promptly!'

'Cesare would have used the information in his own

way,' the Contessa said haltingly.

'You mean there are more ways than one of being a blackmailer?' Amanda sighed. 'I know what you mean exactly!'

'I was afraid Cesare would put pressure on Piero to break his engagement. Cesare is as unscrupulous as Giulio—in his own way.'

'You can say that again!'

The Contessa sighed. 'I will be honest, my darling. I did not think Piero was right for you, but I wanted you to find out for yourself, as you have done, without outside influence. The older I get the more I realise that we only learn from our own experience, never from other people's.'

Amanda had been thinking hard. 'I don't believe it, anyway,' she said suddenly.

The Contessa was bewildered. 'Don't believe what, my dear?'

'I don't believe Piero ever had anything to do with Tina. I've seen them together, and there's no awareness between them. I don't believe Tina is interested in him, nor he in her. Cesare now ... that I would believe! Tina is very aware of him.'

The Contessa frowned. 'Giulio claimed he had proof ... letters, photographs .. Piero promised to marry Tina.'

'Have you asked Piero?' Amanda demanded.

'No, of course not. I haven't mentioned it to him!'

'Then don't you think you should?'

The Contessa looked startled. 'But ...'

'He has the right to know what's being said about him, especially since it has cost you so dearly already!'

'He will be furious!'

'I should just hope so,' Amanda said firmly.

The Contessa pressed her thin hands to her face. 'If it is all a lie I have sacrificed my treasures for nothing!'

'When Cesare hears of it he'll throw Giulio and Tina out of the city for good, and just as well, too! They deserve horse-whipping for the suffering they've caused you!'

'I've been a fool,' the Contessa realised weakly.

'You did what you did for love,' Amanda soothed her. 'No one could blame you for that. You've been tricked by two clever rogues into parting with some valuable objects—but remember, dear Aunt, material possessions weigh lightly in the scale of human values. Cesare knows that.'

The door opened on the words and he appeared. 'What does Cesare know? Apart from the fact that you two bad girls have apparently not been resting, as ordered, but chattering like magpies together? I suppose that that is what women call a rest?'

'It is what we find relaxing sometimes,' Amanda admitted with a dimpled grin.

He flicked one of her ringlets. 'You admit it! That is something, I suppose!'

The open door proved a magnet. Magdalen appeared framed in it, smiling at them, with Piero at her shoulder. 'How are you both feeling now?' she asked them in a friendly fashion. 'You certainly have more colour in your cheeks, Amanda. I was terrified when you fainted like that. You looked like a ghost.'

'That is what she is,' said Piero. 'The ghost of Beatrice.'

His joke was not well received. Cesare glared at him icily

'Is that a stab at me, by any chance?'

Piero flushed. 'No, of course not. I merely meant ... oh, it was just a humorous remark!'

'Not funny,' Cesare commented.

'Amanda must change now,' said the Contessa. 'Come, we will all leave her.'

As she went, Amanda heard her say quietly, 'Piero, I must speak to you ...'

Magdalen followed them. Cesare stood, holding the door and looking at Amanda broodingly. 'You need some food inside you. Hurry and change, then come down to eat.'

She lay on the bed, waiting for him to go. His eyes ran over the slight, frail length of her body. She saw the dark flame light in his gaze, and for a second her heart seemed to stop. Then Cesare had slammed himself out of the room, as if afraid of what he would do if he stayed a moment longer.

She lay there, quivering, fighting down the weakness his look had produced in her. At last she stood up and went to change.

She was dressed, wearing a simple white cotton dress, when the Contessa suddenly returned, her face pale. Amanda turned and looked at her questioningly.

'What did Piero say?'

'He was so angry, Manda *mia* ... he told me he had had a flirtation with Tina several years ago, when he was only just out of his teens, but it had been a mild and brief affair of which he was not ashamed. The rest was lies! He has gone now to see Tina ... he is beside himself with rage. I'm afraid of what he will do to her, to Giulio. He swore terribly! He said I was half-witted to listen to them, that I should have told Cesare or told himself ... he blames me as much as them ...'

'Was Cesare there when you told Piero?'

'No, I thought it best to be discreet. We were alone.'

'But you have told Cesare now?'

'No,' the Contessa admitted. 'Do you think I should?'

Amanda moved to the door rapidly. 'May I tell him? You've had enough shouting for one day! Stay here and rest. I'll see that Cesare stops Piero from doing something drastic!'

The Contessa slumped on to the bed. Amanda left the room and went in search of Cesare. She found him in the tower office, talking on the telephone. He glanced at her quickly as she entered the room, but went on with his business discussion. Amanda bent over and whispered in his ear, 'I must talk to you *now*.'

Cesare looked irritated, but he ended his telephone conversation and looked at her. 'Well? What is so urgent?'

She told him crisply in a calm fashion. Cesare listened without interrupting, his brow gradually darkening to a heavy frown. When she had finished he swore comprehensively, leapt up and strode to the door. She ran after him, clutching at his arm.

'Cesare, don't lose your temper...'

'Don't what?' He almost bared his teeth at her, his eyes black with rage. 'Woman, keep out of this! Women have caused enough trouble as it is! Woolly thinking and clouded emotionalism! My God, there is going to be a reckoning for this! Giulio will think himself lucky if he escapes without being strangled! How dare he! Blackmail my mother! I'll kill him...'

She clung to him apprehensively. 'Please, don't do anything violent!'

A devil seemed to be leaping mercilessly in the grey eyes. He turned upon her a look that froze the blood in her veins. 'Don't talk to me of violence! I have been civilised and restrained for far too long. It is time there was some violence!'

With a twist of his arm he flung her off and stalked away. Amanda hesitated, wondering whether to follow him or to go back to the Contessa. But if she did rejoin the Contessa, what could she tell her which would comfort her? She would bear nothing but ill tidings to her aunt. She decided instead to hurry after Cesare in the hope of averting, somehow, the worst of the brewing storm.

As she fled down the street after Cesare's striding figure she became aware of stares and curious exclamations. Even in her modern dress she was now recognisable, she realised, with a sinking heart. How long would it take to live down that ghastly pageant?

'Hi, Beatrice ... hey, can I take a snap of you?' A cheerful young American hailed her.

She smiled sweetly at him, but pretended not to understand English. She scurried past him and dived down a dark alley which led directly to Giulio's shop. Ahead of her Cesare still strode, oblivious of the interest their progress aroused in the citizens who knew them both.

As they drew nearer to the antique shop Amanda heard muffled sounds which alarmed her. The closer she came the louder the sounds grew until she was certain what they were...

She was hearing angry shouting and the smashing of fragile objects!

A small crowd had gathered already outside Giulio's shop. They backed slightly as Cesare approached, scenting both danger to themselves and an escalation of the exciting violence.

Cesare glared at them. 'Have you nothing better to do than gape there all day?' he demanded ferociously.

They uneasily moved back under his stare, like sheep under the eyes of a wolf, but as soon as Cesare had stalked into the shop they scurried back to hear what happened.

Amanda, arriving a moment later, squeezed her way to the front of the crowd and vanished inside the shop, too. A whisper ran round the crowd as they watched her.

Giulio and Piero were in the back of the shop, out of view of the crowd outside, although their voices were loud enough to explain what was going on between them. Broken glass and china lay scattered around the floor. Giulio was white and tense, and Piero was looking more like Cesare than she had ever seen him look. His handsome face was tougher and more masculine. His eyes were chips of ice.

'You low-down, sneaking bastard!' he snarled at Giulio. 'I'm going to break your neck!'

'That is my privilege, I think,' Cesare drawled, stepping forward.

Piero shot him a look. Giulio began to wear a desperate air. One Druetso was bad enough; two of them was too much to swallow. Piero said tautly, 'Look, Cesare, keep out of this. It is my affair. This piece of flotsam used me as a lever to get the things out of Mamma.'

'But she's my mother, too,' said Cesare. 'I have a right to join in, don't I?'

'Can't you let me handle anything on my own? I'm capable of sorting out Giulio, don't you worry . . .'

'I am the defender of the family honour, not you,' Cesare said. 'You forget that!'

'Forget it? Who could forget it? With that damned hawk everywhere we look . . . on the seal, in the paintings, on the walls, in the tapestries . . . the whole of San Volenco is dominated by you and your damned symbol of authority! How could anyone forget you, Cesare?'

They faced each other belligerently, looking oddly alike. Amanda watched as Giulio, taking advantage of their absorption, began to creep away on tiptoe.

Then she said cheerfully, 'He's sneaking off, boys!'

The two Druetso men swung as one and lunged for

him. Cesare caught him by the left arm, Piero by the right. Cesare grinned at his brother.

'So what shall we do with this rat?'

'Throw him and his girl-friend out of the city for good,' Piero nodded.

'You can't do that,' Giulio protested feebly. 'This is my shop, my antiques ... my livelihood...'

'You can sell the shop and the contents,' said Cesare. 'You're welcome to the value of them. But you will get out of the city and not come back—or I will personally bounce you all the way back to Florence.'

'You can't do it,' Giulio screamed.

'Do you want to be prosecuted for blackmail?'

'There's no evidence against me,' Giulio said in sheer desperation, his eyes narrowed. 'I did nothing illegal!'

'The publicity would kill your business, though, wouldn't it, my dear Giulio?' said Cesare.

Giulio was bitterly silent, and Cesare grinned. 'I give you three days to get out of the city. You can put your goods in the hands of Signor Carizzi—he will handle the sale and see you get a fair price. There is no need for you ever to visit Volenco again.'

'What about the things that lout broke?' Giulio demanded, looking down with fury at the shattered pieces of glass and china. 'Some of them were exquisite, irreplaceable! I've lost a fortune with them alone...'

'Accidents will happen,' Cesare said with a shrug. 'It was only to be expected if you insisted on fighting with Piero!'

'I fight with him! He fought with me! He burst in

here and smashed those things quite callously, like the barbarian he is! He should be shot!'

'Perhaps you can stick them together,' Piero said with a grin.

Giulio stamped his foot like a child in a temper. 'Don't be absurd! You insult me! That would not give me back my lovely things...'

'Nor can you give my mother back her lovely things,' said Cesare starkly.

Giulio had the grace to look confused. 'That is different! She had the money for them...'

'Money? Is that all these things mean to you, you shark? My mother cares nothing for the money. To her those objects were priceless, and you made her sell them!' Cesare was angry again now, his eyes full of biting contempt. 'I ought to break your neck for what you did!'

Suddenly Tina whirled into the shop, her face flushed and angry. 'What is going on here? Giulio, what is all this?' She stared around the shop, taking in the broken fragments, the angry faces of the men, Amanda's silent, watchful presence. 'Giulio, what is happening here?'

He looked at her sulkily. 'Ask them!'

'The game is up,' Cesare said tersely.

Piero looked at her contemptuously. 'You lying little cat! If I never see you in Volenco again it will be too soon...'

Tina understood at once—her expression told them as much. She looked around the circle from face to face, her eyes defiant and hard. 'So! Someone talked too much.

The Contessa, eh? Sentimental old fool!' She stared at Amanda. 'To you, I suppose? She was always soft about you! Well, don't expect me to go down on my knees and beg!'

'Tina!' Giulio looked at her warningly. 'There must be some other way out,' he said in a pleading tone to Cesare. 'We belong here! We are members of the family! Where will we go? What will we do?'

'We'll make money,' Tina said violently, grabbing him by the arm and shaking him. 'Don't beg them for anything, Giulio. Kick their teeth in ... don't kneel! We will go to Milan and sell antiques. We will be rich and independent. No more medieval systems ... no more slavery. We will take what we want and be happy.'

Cesare eyed her thoughtfully, then he looked at Giulio. 'If I were you I would watch her! I see a touch of Lady Macbeth there!' He turned and walked off, followed by Piero and Amanda after a brief pause.

Amanda glanced back and saw Giulio and Tina facing each other in silence, a wintry resignation on Giulio's face, but sullen defiance on Tina's. What sort of life would they make together? she asked herself. She was glad she did not have to face such armed hostility.

As they walked back up towards the castle, dark clouds began to bank up in the west, and a powerful wind sprung up, blowing them fast towards the rearing bulk of the city on its mountain.

'Looks like a bad night,' Cesare murmured, looking up.

'Lucky we had the Beatrice pageant when we did,'

Piero said with a nod.

Cesare glanced at him. 'I hope Magdalen does not hear about Tina, or your goose is cooked for good, my boy.'

'Don't be hypocritical,' Piero snapped. 'You would like that very much. You hate Magdalen and her father.'

'Only because he doesn't understand them,' Amanda ventured softly.

Cesare gave her a grim look. 'What do you know about it? Keep out of the discussion.'

'I know why they bought Mireze,' she said.

'So do I,' Cesare ground out. 'To infuriate me. And they succeeded.'

'They bought it as a wedding present for Piero,' Amanda told him sweetly.

There was a tense silence. She watched Cesare. He looked quite blank for a while, then he swore beneath his breath with great savagery.

'Why didn't they say so long ago?'

'Did you give them a chance?'

'They could have made me listen,' Cesare said irritably.

'They have their pride, too, you know. It is not the exclusive prerogative of Italians.'

'What a piece of stupidity! To ruin so many lives for pride's sake...'

'Oh; Cesare,' she exclaimed disbelievingly, 'Piero is right—you are a hypocrite!'

He glared at her. 'What?'

But at that moment the heavens opened and the rain began to pour down upon them in torrents. Ducking their heads against it, they ran for the door and dashed inside, just as the generator failed and all the lights went out.

Cesare began to laugh helpleslsy. 'No one can say this has not been an eventful day!'

'Where are the candles?' Amanda gasped, brushing the rain from her face with a handkerchief. 'I must go up and change yet again—my clothes are saturated.'

Cesare fumbled in the dark, produced a candle, found matches and lit it. The small flame made a brave attempt against the engulfing dark, but it was only able to push it back a short space. Cesare lit another, handed Amanda one. Piero disappeared without waiting for a candle, and Cesare lifted his candle. 'Shall I light you up the stairs, Manda?'

She would have liked to refuse his offer, but she hated the dark on her own. 'Thank you,' she whispered, aware of the huge bulk of the stone building pressing down upon them. On just such a night as this had she arrived back here, to thunder and lightning, and she climbed the stairs fearfully, listening to the wind blowing out the tapestries and whistling down the chimneys. Lightning flashed outside the windows. The old building seemed to be beset by invisible armies.

Amanda looked at Cesare's broad shoulders ahead of her. The pale candlelight just showed her the shape of his dark head. She found his presence inexpressibly comforting, and her need and reliance on him made her confused and resentful. What price independence and pride if it could all be overthrown by the alarum of a thunderstorm? She desired to be free, yet found herself constantly seeking Cesare's protection and support. It was maddening.

At the door of her room, Cesare paused and looked down at her. She saw the bold hawk-like profile, then looked away, her heart thudding.

'Thank you for today,' he said softly.

'Today?'

'The pageant,' he smiled.

Amanda laughed. 'Oh, so much has happened since then that I'd forgotten it.'

'I shall never forget it,' he said deeply. 'You were all that I had dreamed you could be ... my Beatrice...'

She knew that he was going to kiss her, and her whole body yearned for the touch of his mouth, but she forced herself to step away quickly.

'It was nothing,' she said hurriedly. 'I'm so wet. I must change now ... thank you for lighting me upstairs, Cesare...'

The door closed between them. She leant against it, shuddering, and above the thunder of her own breathing heard Cesare slowly move away. Even with the door between them she could sense the repressed passion in him, almost hear the turmoil of his blood.

What am I to do? she asked the darkness. Can I go on like this, holding him off, fighting my own love as well as his? She recalled what he had said to her recently ... that he was not made of steel! Would he break? Or would it be herself who broke under this unbearable pressure?

CHAPTER TEN

HER dreams that night were vivid and nightmarish. She dreamt she was walking through a wood, the dark wood of the Botticelli painting, but now it was filtered with sunshine and at her feet flowered primroses and violets, English flowers of the spring, their fragrance drifting upwards to her nostrils, making her feel gay and optimistic. Then suddenly the sunshine vanished. A cloud hung over the trees, casting gloom not only over the landscape but over her spirits. She looked down and the flowers, too, had gone. The grass was withering, the leaves began to fall.

She cried aloud in astonishment, putting out her hands. A brown leaf fell on to the palm of one of them; she felt the crisp dry texture on her skin. Under her gaze it became skeletal until it lay like a cobweb on her hand. She shrank in horror and it dropped off.

It was so strange, so menacing, to see the normal course of the seasons suddenly escalate like this, that she stared around her in terror of what she would next find.

She saw a figure moving through the bare, black trees towards her. It was Cesare. His dark head was unmistakable. He was, oddly, wearing his magnificent Renaissance costume, the black and silver cloak flaring out from his broad shoulders. The silver ribbons glinted in the moonlight.

Moonlight? Amanda looked up at the dark sky. How had night come so fast?

Cesare was coming slowly towards her. She ran to meet him, putting out her hands in welcome, then stopped dead as she saw that her fingers were bony, shrivelled, the pale skin loose upon them.

I'm old, she thought. I am ageing, like the wood. Something terrible has happened to me.

She put her hands over her face, terrified that Cesare should see her like this, and sobbed violently ... 'No, no ... don't look ... go away!'

Then suddenly she was staring with wide, petrified eyes at daylight, and she was awake in her bedroom.

She lay trembling for a moment, reliving the horror of the dream. What a strange thing to dream! A nightmare! It's odd, she thought—I've never been afraid of growing old before. Why should I dream that?

She sat up, absorbed and intent, staring at the clock on the table.

It ticked rhythmically away, second by second, minute by minute, hour by hour; a machine, tireless, emotionless, unaware of itself or anything else.

But human beings are neither machines nor emotionless. They, too, measure time, but the passing of time has meaning for them.

'That's what my dream meant,' she whispered huskily to herself. 'I'm young now. It's my spring. But one day, all too soon, I shall be old, and then I shall have lost my chance of fulfilment ...'

Gather ye rosebuds while ye may, she remembered

confusedly. All those old proverbs! Make hay while the sun shines. The known truths of the human race enshrined in a few words, but becoming so mossy with age and use that they are hardly respected any longer.

I should have known, she told herself. If I resist Cesare I'm resisting my own chance of happiness. I love him—why not admit it? He loves me. I must be mad if I keep on running away from him like this...

He'll tyrannise over me, she reminded herself. He will expect me to be his wife, first and foremost—a housewife, a mother. Cesare has no belief in women's aspirations. He's been brought up an autocrat, accustomed to command and be obeyed. He's ruthless. He's merciless.

I love him, she thought, her passion swamping every other consideration, and I want him...

She leapt out of bed, hurriedly washed and dressed in her jodhpurs and a clean blue shirt, and went down to the stables to join him for their usual ride.

Tina was in the stables, sullenly moving about in the tackroom, her eyes dark-ringed. She glared at Amanda and said nothing. Then Cesare emerged from the kitchen, flicking his crop at his boots, an aloof expression on his handsome face. 'Have you saddled the horses?' he asked Carlo, the thin lad who helped around the stables for sheer love of horses.

'I did it,' Tina put in defiantly. 'It will be the last time I ever look after Vesta...' Her glance at the mare was almost pathetic in its intensity.

Cesare shrugged. He turned and lifted Amanda to the saddle. His hands lingered on her waist, as though reluctant to release her. She looked down into his dark face and their eyes met with the impact of a violent collision at high speed. She felt the jar throughout her body.

Cesare's eyes widened, a hungry flame shot into them. She saw his lips shape her name.

But then he visibly controlled his passion, turned away and leapt into the saddle.

At that instant Tina burst into a shriek of spiteful laughter, and Volenco Viva reared up, his front feet clawing the air, a desperate whinny of rage and pain breaking from him.

'What have you done, you little hellcat?' Cesare demanded of Tina as he strove desperately to stay on Viva's back. The horse plunged and kicked, twisting himself in apparent agony.

'Jump,' Amanda begged Cesare. 'Dearest, jump off now ...'

Too late. The stallion had grown too desperate. He shot off at a gallop, with Cesare clinging desperately to him, his lean face grimly set.

'What is it?' Amanda asked Tina angrily. 'What did you do?'

'Wouldn't you like to know?' Tina retorted. 'You'll be lucky if your precious Cesare comes back alive! I hope Viva kills him. I hope he kicks his head in ... I'd laugh at the funeral!'

Amanda turned her mare and followed in Viva's wake, her features white as Tina's words sank home. Cesare might be killed before she had had the chance to tell him . . . to show him . . . She winced. The nightmare was coming true.

People were anxiously hurrying down the city streets, having seen Cesare shoot by on Viva's back. They called to her in high Italian. 'He was going so fast . . .'

'The horse bolted with him?' they called as she rode past. Amanda nodded, wasting no words. She could not have spoken. Her throat appeared to be as dry as ashes.

When she rode through the gate she saw Cesare disappearing into the vineyards at a tremendous pace. She galloped after him, her heart pounding. What had Tina done to make Viva behave like that?

It was totally alien to the stallion's nature to be so vicious. He had always been high-spirited, it was true, but he had never turned on his master. There was genuine rapport between horse and master. Amanda had always found it moving to see the great, powerful animal nibble at Cesare's ear adoringly. Moving—and maddening. She had resented the fact that Cesare could so easily charm the stallion, the people of the city and apparently every woman he met. It was not fair that a man should have that sort of charm, especially when he had so many other attributes.

She found herself ducking and weaving through the vines. Men came running towards her, shouting and pointing, their faces grave. She sensed what they said, although the words were muffled at this distance, and her heart seemed to stop.

Cesare had been thrown!

Please, God, she prayed desperately, don't let him be

killed. Please, please, not Cesare...

She saw Viva, running with sweat, his coat matted, his eyes rolling in his head, standing by a fence, his sides heaving visibly. A few feet away, arms flung wide, lay Cesare. Ominously still, she realised, as she rode up and flung herself down from Vesta's back. Already several men were kneeling beside him, but they drew back respectfully as she ran towards them.

'Is he conscious?' she asked breathlessly.

'No, *signorina*...' they told her. 'Giacomo has gone to the vineyard office to telephone for the doctor,' they informed her politely.

Amanda knelt beside Cesare and looked at his face. He had his eyes shut. There was a cut on his forehead and dark blood trickled from it. His skin looked very pale beside his black hair. She lifted one of his hands, felt carefully for the pulse at his wrist. It seemed very faint. Her own heart missed a beat. How badly was he hurt?

She felt helpless, useless, not knowing what to do. One of the men asked her gently, 'Shall we carry him to the office?'

'No,' she said. 'He must not be moved. It's dangerous to move someone until you know for certain how serious their injuries are! The doctor will come and tell us.'

As if he heard her voice there was the sound of a car racing along the road through the vineyards, and a few moments later the young doctor puffed up to them, his face anxious. He nodded to her. 'He had a fall from his horse, I understand?'

'Yes. He's unconscious,' she said miserably. 'We didn't

move him in case of injury . . .'

The doctor gave her an approving smile. 'Good. Very wise.'

He knelt down and deftly began to examine Cesare, his thin fingers oddly delicate as they moved over the long body. Amanda watched with her heart in her mouth. This is a punishment for my folly, she thought. If he dies . . . I've wasted my chance of happiness.

'He has a broken rib,' the doctor announced after a time. 'Really, he is as usual unbelievably fortunate! How many times I've known him take incredible risks and come up smiling! One day his luck will run out, though, so he should start to be more careful.'

'But his head,' Amanda whispered, pointing to the cut. 'And he's unconscious!'

'Yes, he may have concussion,' the doctor agreed. 'But that is something we will only find out when he wakes up. He must go to hospital, of course. He will have to be X-rayed. He may have internal injuries I cannot find.' His thoughtful glance rested on Cesare's head.

She shivered. 'Can I go with him?'

The doctor glanced at her. 'Why not? There will be nothing for you to do, though. You realise that? You will have to sit in the waiting-room and wait, perhaps for hours. Wouldn't you rather go back and comfort the Contessa?'

'Others may do that,' she said fiercely. 'She has Piero and Aunt Teresa . . . Cesare needs me.'

The doctor shrugged. 'As you like.'

One of the vineyard workers slid up to Amanda as she waited to climb into the ambulance beside Cesare. 'I took a look at the horse,' he whispered. 'This was under the saddle.'

She took the thing he held out to her, and gave a groan of angry protest. It was a small metal object she recognised. It came from a collection of medieval torture instruments kept in a glass case in the castle. This one was used, as Tina had used it, to drive horses mad and make them turn upon their riders. It was a porcupine, made of iron, and spots of blood showed where it had dug into Viva's flesh. Cesare's weight on the saddle, of course, had forced the ghastly thing down into the horse's back, making Viva desperate to get rid of his rider.

'Tina . . .' she breathed. 'How vile . . . how wicked!'

The vineyard workers made a low hissing sound of rage. One of them was holding Viva's bridle. The stallion was looking unhappy and dispirited. Amanda went up to him and gently stroked his long nose. 'No one blames you, poor darling,' she murmured. 'Least of all Cesare! It wasn't your fault . . .'

Then the doctor asked if she was ready, so she turned away and climbed into the ambulance, taking her seat beside Cesare, holding his chilled fingers between her own, gently rubbing them as if she might put back the natural body warmth into them by doing so.

The ambulance carried them to the hospital some miles across the other side of the plain. It was a small rural hospital, of course, but there was a reassuring warmth about the reception they got. Cesare was X-rayed, then wheeled back to the small side-ward in which he was to sleep. Amanda was permitted to go in later, when he was in bed, to see him for a few moments. He was still unconscious, his skin drained and colourless against the crisp white pillow.

'We have not got the result of the X-rays yet, but when we do I will let you know at once,' the doctor assured her.

'Thank you. How do you think he looks?' she begged.

'His pulse is getting stronger. You can't say for certain until he recovers consciousness, but I don't think, somehow, that there is anything drastically wrong. Of course, that is pure guesswork, but I know Cesare. He is fit and very strong. It would take more than a fall from a horse to kill him.'

'I hope you're right.'

'I hope so too,' the doctor assured her.

'Can I stay for a while?'

'It would not be wise. He will be watched, don't worry. A nurse will be in here all the time. You had far better go and get yourself some food.'

'I couldn't eat!'

'Some coffee, then,' the doctor insisted. 'You need some nourishment—you've had a shock. I tell you what, come along to my office, and I'll give you something to lessen the impact of the shock.'

She obeyed him reluctantly, took two little red pills and a cup of milky coffee laced with sugar and, she suspected, brandy. Then she resumed her vigil outside Cesare's room.

She only left her post once during the next few hours. She went to the powder-room to wash and freshen up, then rang San Volenco with the latest bulletin. The Contessa was lying down, having contracted a migraine after the shock of hearing the news, but Piero spoke to Amanda reassuringly. 'She is tougher than she looks, you know. She will weather this—so long as Cesare is going to be all right.'

'I'm sure he is,' Amanda promised. 'They are all very soothing here. I know a lot of it's standard hospital practice, but under that I feel they're genuinely confident. The X-rays were quite satisfactory, they say. No sign of internal injury.'

'And the head? Did they X-ray his head?'

'Oh, yes, they seem sure that his head injury is superficial, but the unconsciousness is worrying, of course. Until he regains consciousness they won't be one hundred per cent certain about brain damage.'

Piero sighed. 'Well, we must hope ...'

'Is Magdalen there?' asked Amanda.

'Yes, do you wish to speak to her?'

'Please, just for a moment!'

Magdalen spoke within seconds, proof that she had been beside Piero, listening intently. Amanda spoke to her affectionately.

'Try to cheer Piero up! He's fond of Cesare, you know, underneath his rebellious outbursts.'

Magdalen's voice was warm. 'Don't worry, I'll do my best.'

'I hope you have come together again,' Amanda said on a sigh. 'I would like to think that you two, at least, have made up your differences.'

'And you will have the chance to do the same with Cesare very soon,' said Magdalen, understanding why Amanda sounded so sad.

Amanda sighed again. 'I could kick myself for wasting so much time! So many years...'

Later, resuming her vigil outside his room, she thought back over those years of exile in England, and realised that she had not been mature enough at eighteen to cope with the demands Cesare would have made upon her. She had done the only thing possible when she fled from him. She had needed time to grow up, time to reach understanding of her own needs as well as his. They had been better apart during those years.

A click made her turn her head alertly. The young nurse smiled at her gravely, her olive-skinned face slightly flushed with excitement.

'He is awake, *signorina* ... I have buzzed for the doctors, but I think you could see him for a moment before they arrive ... he seems drowsy but aware of his surroundings.' She smiled again, her eyes amused. 'He even asked after his horse!'

Amanda followed her back into the room hastily, her knees shaking.

Cesare lay against the pillows, his eyes now wide open, his gaze fixed on the door as they entered.

She sank to her knees beside the bed and reached for his nearest hand. 'Cesare . . .'

He looked at her, smiling faintly, a great light buried deep within those grey eyes, eyes which held no coldness for her now. 'Did I give you a shock, my darling?'

'A hell of a shock,' she said, with an abrupt laugh.

He grinned, well satisfied, reading between the lines with his usual quick intelligence. 'Well, that's something,' he murmured. 'This bang on the head will have been worth it if that's the case.'

She blushed, aware that he was too quick for her. 'Does your head hurt?'

'Horribly,' he said, beginning to turn on the pillow, then gave a groan and clutched at his bandaged chest. 'What the hell have I done to this?'

'Don't try to move,' the nurse protested. 'You have a broken rib.'

The doctors were at the door, giving the nurse reproving looks as they saw Amanda in the room. She bent and kissed Cesare very lightly on the cheek.

'I must go for now,' she said. 'I'll see you later.'

He caught her hand, lifted it slowly to his lips and kissed her palm with lingering passion. Very pink and agitated, she withdrew her hand and walked to the door.

The young doctor from Volenco followed her while his hospital colleagues examined Cesare.

'I'm afraid you will not be able to see him again tonight,' he told her kindly. 'He will be sleeping. You must go back to Volenco and come again tomorrow afternoon.'

'Oh, no,' she protested.

'Yes,' he nodded. 'Don't worry. We will be in touch if anything goes wrong, but although I still can't be certain I am more than ever convinced that he is going to be fine. We will have to keep him in here for a while, of course. Head injuries are always suspect, especially after unconsciousness like this, but the X-rays were good, and he seems quite rational. We shall see...'

She had to accept this verdict. The doctor drove her back to Volenco himself, since he had already spent more time than he could afford on the case. He spent two afternoons a week at the hospital, normally, he explained, since he was able to follow up his own cases personally there. 'I'm no expert on head injuries, but they have a good man in the hospital. You know, he has a nose for serious cases, and he was quite optimistic about Cesare, too. I trust his judgment.'

The Contessa and Piero met her in the hall, their faces anxious. Aunt Teresa was softly weeping in the background. She always expected the worst.

'He's going to be fine,' Amanda assured them.

'You have seen him?' asked the Contessa.

'Yes, and he was already getting restless,' Amanda smiled. 'I'm glad I'm not nursing him. He'll be a terror to those nurses!'

The Contessa sighed. 'At least he has recovered consciousness. That frightened me, the long lapse of time when he was unconscious.'

Amanda nodded grimly. 'Me, too. I prayed hard during the hours I waited outside that room. But I knew when I saw him that he was going to be all right. It was in his face. He was still drowsy, still a bit weak, but there was a definite improvement since the last time I saw him. He had slightly more colour.'

'That wicked girl,' the Contessa said grimly. 'To do such a thing! It is inconceivable! But she has paid...'

Amanda looked enquiringly at them. Piero told her, 'The vineyard workers came into the city to find her—and they were pretty rough. She and Giulio fled in panic. I think they narrowly escaped being killed.'

Amanda nodded. 'And Viva? How is Viva? Cesare's first question was about Viva.'

'How like him,' Piero muttered. 'Viva will be all right in a few days. The porcupine does no permanent damage, you know.'

'It has damaged Viva's confidence in human beings,' Amanda said gravely.

They all looked unhappy for a while, then Magdalen came down to join them, her expression tentative, as if she was not sure of her welcome. Amanda smiled at her.

'Hello! Come and talk to me while I get ready for bed. I'm worn out.'

'I will send up a meal to your room,' the Contessa said at once.

'Thank you,' said Amanda gratefully. 'I'm starving ... I couldn't eat at the hospital, I was too worried.'

The Contessa smiled lovingly at her. 'My dearest child,' she murmured. 'I am so glad.'

Amanda knew that there was no need for words between them. The Contessa already knew that Amanda had stopped running away from Cesare. She had known it at once on setting eyes on her. There was a joyous light in the still beautiful eyes. The Contessa knew that her dearest wish was about to come true, and, despite Cesare's accident, she was ecstatically happy.

Magdalen perched on the end of the bed and grinned impishly at Amanda as she slid between the sheets.

'Do I hear the distant sound of wedding bells?'

'Don't we both?' Amanda parried.

Magdalen shrugged. 'Don't suggest a double wedding —on my wedding day I'm going to be the only bride around! I've been dreaming of this for years.' A rapt expression crept over her face. 'White suits me, you see ... I thought ivory satin, cut very simply but exquisitely ... with a pearl headdress and a very long flowing veil ... I'm going to have my shoes made in Milan. They make the best shoes in the world. They make your feet look half the size, yet they're ultra-comfortable!'

Amanda laughed. 'I see you've got it planned to the last detail! What is Piero to wear? Do you need any bridesmaids?'

'Do you think Cesare will wait long enough?' Magdalen teased. 'He doesn't look the patient sort.'

'He's waited five years!'

Magdalen groaned. 'Just as well he's tucked up safely in a hospital bed. We might just have time to squeeze our wedding in before they let him loose.'

'Oh, he must be there,' Amanda said, looking shocked.

'Do you think he'll allow it?' asked Magdalen doubtfully.

'Of course he will,' Amanda promised, and Magdalen went off to bed looking hopeful.

Amanda was shocked and dismayed when, next morning, the Contessa told her that Cesare had ordered that she should not visit him again.

'Why not?' she asked unhappily.

'He said something about not wanting you to take him out of pity,' the Contessa smiled.

'What nonsense,' Amanda said at once. 'I shall go, whatever he says.'

'I told him you would say that,' said the Contessa. 'He told me to tell you he would refuse to see you if you turned up there. He was adamant. My dear, you know what he is like in one of these moods!'

'The autocrat to his fingertips,' agreed Amanda crossly. 'He can't do this!'

'It won't be for long,' the Contessa soothed.

It seemed, however, like an eternity to Amanda as she waited day after day, hearing news of him at second hand from the Contessa and Piero.

She and Magdalen were able to keep busy in planning Magdalen and Piero's wedding, which was to take place at Mireze, as tradition dictated. The church at Mireze was adorable, a very small stone building with famous stained glass windows and some exquisite statuary around the walls.

Magdalen had her wedding dress, like her shoes, made in Milan, to the disgust of Signora Marella. Amanda promised her faithfully that she should make *her* wedding dress.

'If the day ever comes when I need one,' she added discreetly.

Signora Marella gave her an amused look. 'Of course,' she agreed, tongue in cheek. 'For you I think silk and tulle ... very innocent and floating ... ethereal, spiritual ...' An ecstatic look filled her dark face. 'Ah, it will be the best thing I ever made! Every woman in the city will be mad with envy! They will hate me...'

Amanda laughed. 'You're shocking me!'

Magdalen said, 'You're making me regret I didn't ask you to make mine! How was I to know you were a whizz, Signora Marella?'

Later, she and Piero drove off with Magdalen's father to see the stables at Mireze. Piero had agreed to take over control of them after his marriage. Cesare had been consulted, and had, reluctantly, agreed, although he had said he would miss his brother's help in the Druetso estates.

Amanda sat in the sunny walled garden, her eyes contentedly closed, enjoying the warm fragrance of the flowers. She could hear one bird repeatedly chinking in the ivy. Out on the blue swell of the sky were a few larks, riding the warm currents of air above the plain, their song soaring heavenward.

Then someone stood between her and the sun, and a flower was drawn lightly across her lips. She remembered another occasion when, with closed lids, she had invited a kiss, and her heart beat frantically against her ribs.

It couldn't be, she thought, keeping her eyes shut tight. She waited a moment, then whispered huskily, 'Cesare?'

He did not move. The kiss she was longing for did not fall on her raised lips.

She opened her eyes. He was very big and dark, almost appearing to tower over her. Amanda felt her body weaken at the sight of him, a feeling of lassitude and yearning invading her.

When their eyes met his held hers commandingly, searching their depths as if trying to penetrate her thoughts, to read her heart with merciless intent.

Suddenly she knew that, after so long a pursuit, the hunter demanded the full capitulation of his quarry. Without a word, Cesare was requiring of her total surrender. He did not mean to meet her halfway. There was to be no chivalrous understanding on this occasion. Cesare's male pride demanded that she make the first move this time.

She had abandoned her pride long ago. It had crumbled when she saw him so white and vulnerable at her feet in the vineyards. There was only room for love in her heart now.

She lifted her arms, clinging to his neck, and kissed him with unleashed hunger. For a moment Cesare stood unresponsive under her kiss, then he gave a stifled groan and caught her to him, his hands like steel on her waist.

'At last,' he whispered against her mouth. 'I've got you ... you'll never escape me again, my dove ... the hawk has his claws in you at last, and you are really done for.'

She laughed breathlessly, caressing his hair and the back of his strong neck. 'It's what I want, don't you see, it's what I have always wanted, but now I'm no longer afraid to admit it. I'm yours, Cesare. I only want you to love me.'

His hands moved slowly, possessively over her body, arousing in her feelings she had only guessed at until now. She groaned and clung to him, and heard him laugh softly before his mouth came down again to devour her lips, parting them ruthlessly, bruising them with the unleashed hunger of years.

Then he suddenly withdrew and buried his face in her neck, his skin burning hot against her cool flesh. She heard him whisper hoarsely, 'Manda, I'm almost afraid ... I want you so much ... I'm afraid to touch you. I've waited so long, I'm almost out of my mind with desire. Suddenly you're here, in my arms, wanting me back, and I'm frightened of my own emotions. You don't know how much I want you.'

'I want you, too, darling,' she told him tenderly.

He groaned. 'You're too innocent to know. I'm a starving man suddenly given the chance to assuage his hunger. I'm afraid it may slip out of my control ... I'm only human and I want you like hell now, right now.'

She felt her heart pounding desperately as his words sank into her mind. She shook, clinging to him, her own face on fire, her body trembling. 'Cesare, my darling...'

He straightened, taking a deep breath. Then he took her flushed face between both hands, 'There, I'm back on the leash,' he said with grim humour. 'Kiss me.'

She lifted her face eagerly. Their mouths clung for a moment, then he moved back again.

'We must go in and tell my mother to make her plans

for a wedding,' he said. 'It had better be soon or I won't be answerable for my actions.'

'It will be soon,' she promised. 'But not soon enough!'

Cesare laughed and looked up at the strong walls of his home. 'I never thought to hear you say such things, my dearest,' he said triumphantly. 'See, the city is filled with joy tonight.'

The setting sun flooded the whole city with a golden light. It looked as if, as he said, Volenco was rejoicing with them, rejoicing that the Hawk had captured his prize at last.

Have you missed any of these best-selling Harlequin Romances?

By popular demand... to help complete your collection of Harlequin Romances

48 titles listed on the following pages...

Harlequin Reissues

Harlequin Reissues

Complete and mail this coupon today!